THAT TIME OF DAY

SHORT STORIES

GABRIELLA CONTESTABILE

PRAISE FOR "THAT TIME OF DAY"

"It is hard to write something about a book that you love—a book that is light and deep in the same moment, one keeping the quietness and charm of a lullaby, one locked in your heart and to which you return every time we need comfort and love.

"Gabriella takes us by hand through a dreamy trip that touches the most beautiful Italian places, and yet there is nothing unreal or distant in these beautiful stories. You can taste the ingredients of the food and smell the aroma of the coffee, and you find yourself, many times, squinting your eyes as you would do when staring at the most gorgeous sunset in some magic place and hour and location in Italy.

"A beautiful collection of human richness, wonderfully embroidered with the lives and loves of characters, with sadness and regrets, and with never-ending hopes for the future, revealing how beauty is always a savior of our lives, especially when we are prone to despair."

— ANGELA VITALIANO, JOURNALIST &
ACTIVIST

"Once again, Ms. Contestabile has done it. She effort-
lessly takes our senses, emotions and imagination on a
meaningful journey. Like a mirror, Ms. Contestabile's
work reflects the human experience sculpted from
culture and preserved with passion. A must read!"

— DR. MARIE-ELENA LIOTTA,
PRESIDENT ENRICO FERMI EDUCATION
FOUNDATION

"*That Time of Day* is a lyrical homage to Italy,
following each story's protagonist in a life-defining
moment as she returns to Italy or her Italian heritage.
So perfectly does Gabriella bring to life all of the five
senses—sight, sound, smell, taste, and touch. So much
so that I could actually taste the mouthwatering foods
as described. *That Time of Day* is perfect for a sunny
day at the beach or for a wintery evening cuddled up
with your favorite pet and drink."

— SUZANNE HARVEY, LONG TIME
ADVOCATE FOR THE EMPOWERMENT
OF WOMEN AND GIRLS THROUGH UN
WOMEN, FRIENDS OF THE UN, AND
PEACE IN THE STREETS GLOBAL FILM
FESTIVAL

"In *That Time of Day*, Gabriella Contestabile delivers a rare feast of language, story and place, brimming with the essence of family connection, and illuminating how the past tugs at us and dares us to move in different directions...and all with the glories of Italy past and present and the incredible heart and strength of Italian women. *Bravissima! That Time of Day* is a wonderful, literary, and moving read."

— PHYLLIS MELHADO, AUTHOR OF *THE SPA AT LAVENDER LANE* AND CO-AUTHOR OF *CHASING LIFE*

"It is always a pleasure to read stories written by Gabriella Contestabile. The flow of her writing casts a poetic impression, and she brings each scene to life. I find myself experiencing the sights, sounds and sensations as if I were her characters. Her stories capture the female experience—our joys, our sorrows, our regrets—and she always offers her characters, and readers, a ray of hope for a brighter future."

— MARILYN WILSON, FREELANCE WRITER, BOOK REVIEWER, AND AUTHOR OF *THE WISDOM OF LISTENING* AND *LIFE OUTSIDE THE BOX*

THAT TIME OF DAY

Published February 2023

ISBN: 979-8-9871051-6-0

Library of Congress Control Number: 2022922640

For information address:

The Three Tomatoes Publishing

6 Soundview Rd.

Glen Cove, NY 11542

www.thethreetomatoespublishing.com

Cover design: Catherine Michele Adams, Inkslinger Editing

Interior design: Catherine Michele Adams, Inkslinger Editing

To Steve

"It is the hour when the sky has lost its sun but has not yet found its stars."

— *JACQUES GUERLAIN*

CONTENTS

THIS COLLECTION'S BEGINNING

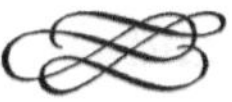

I gathered these stories together during a pandemic lockdown when all we previously assumed was suspended. My mother was ill, and we tended to her, not knowing when the end would be but knowing that it would be soon. We didn't know then, nor do we know now, how the pandemic will end. Within that silence, rendered richer by long walks in nature or along the storied avenues of grand architecture of years past, a volume of histories rose out of the ashes, like the first spring blossoms we pay attention to because for months we've been frozen in time.

Global histories meet personal histories. No longer distracted by social events and preparations for them, experiences curtailed, luxuries left not purchased, we have been forced for over two years to find meaning in emptiness. But in open, unadorned space, our deepest insights can take hold. It's here that we discover those impetuous buds of promise once ignored.

At this crossroads, we are forced, individually, collectively, to delve into the void. And so, Jacques Guerlain's quote came to mind. A representation of the shifting time in which we stand. On a bridge spanning a river, perhaps the Arno, or the Seine, or the Tiber, or even the river that exists in our imagination. Actual or virtual, the sensation is the same. We are held aloft, suspended above the water. We are no longer tethered to our earth. The sky and the air around us darken. The sunset that blazed is now at rest, and for a moment all feels lost. We mourn the day that has passed, an opportunity unexplored, a dream unfulfilled, a hope dashed, a loved one gone. But we stay still. We don't run from where we stand. We listen for the silence. We settle into the echoes and shadows. And then, when the sky is its darkest, we see the stars.

Inside this whispered darkness, the stars emerge at their leisure, one and then a few, and then at once, they burst into sparkles across the heavens. We need loss to see clearly future courses of departure. Before we take flight again with reinforced wings.

GIULIETTA'S PROMISE

Claudia's mother told her that a girl without a good head would always have good feet. That meant that if you didn't think hard enough about what you were doing, you'd mess up and have to retrace your steps to fix it.

Her mother's feet were always moving: on the pedals she pumped at the bathing suit factory in the garment district, up and down the steps of their Forest Hills garden apartment, all around the houses they moved into and out of each time her father lost a job or was stalked by a pregnant mistress.

"Your mother's feet never leave the ground," her father boasted, as if it were his achievement, not hers. Mama's kidskin pumps went where her father's wingtips never ventured: to parent-teacher meetings, to the school lunchroom with forgotten milk money, up and down the front steps to shovel snow while her father was off to "God knows where."

"It was just a cup of coffee, Claudia," he told her over a meager breakfast of toast and butter. "We talked about opera. Your mother is suspicious about everything." Claudia's mother had just discovered he'd been going to Maddalena's every morning before work.

To hide her grimace, Claudia turned to get apricot jam. Would they ever eat cannoli again? Maddalena and her husband owned the pastry shop on Austin Street where Claudia's family bought their daily bread and Sunday pastries. In fact, where would they get that crusty bread, sesame seed studded, made ever more beatific when dipped in the olive oil shipped to them from her grandfather's olive groves in Lucca? At home her mother did what the American moms found barbaric. She poured olive oil from a giant tin into a dish, sliced in tomatoes, and gave Claudia chunks of the still warm bread with crispy edges to mop everything up with. It was so delicious, Claudia was shocked when her friends turned up their noses.

"They'll learn in due time," her mother reassured her. "Someday they'll realize this is so much better than peanut butter on white bread."

Would that they realized it sooner, at least in time for the junior prom. Claudia wanted a date. She wanted also for the grumpy lady at Motor Vehicles to realize that her mother's modestly accented English was actually more correct than her own; that these two foreigners, mother and child, spoke two languages to her one. Instead, a crass boy in mathematics had declared that since she had pierced ears and a name with so many vowels, Claudia should go back to the country she came from.

But her father's worst dalliance would be with Veronica, the sister of Claudia's best friend, Cathy. Petite and curvy Veronica had wide, innocent eyes like the German actress Maria Schell. She put lipstick on with a tiny brush after she'd drawn around the outside with a darker pencil so her lips were as red and as perfect as Marilyn Monroe's. Veronica wore short shorts and ruffled blouses like Ann Margaret in *Bye Bye Birdie*, and her glossy ponytail swung back and forth when she walked.

Cathy never came over again after that. Their walks to school, their sleepovers and hours-long phone conversations about boys they had crushes on—these stopped, too. When they saw each other in school, each turned away. Claudia's face burned whenever she walked into the lunchroom and saw her old friend chatting wildly with the other girls. They stopped their conversations and glared through narrowing eyes. And she knew Cathy had told them. It was one more thing to point to her foreignness, her shame. Their fathers, American fathers like the one in *Father Knows Best,* would not have kissed a seventeen-year-old girl on a park bench in Forest Park.

But worse than this, she missed Cathy. She missed knowing she was always on the other side of the phone when a boy she liked didn't call. She eventually made friends with Thea, one of the new Greek girls who was always on a diet but ate a chocolate and peppermint ice cream pop for lunch every day. Thea never cared what the other girls thought. One evening after dinner, Cathy's mother, who at one time had told Claudia she was the most mature of her daughter's friends, stopped by and, without coming inside, told both Claudia's parents to stay away from her family or she would call the police.

A few nights later her mother, after giving her husband the silent treatment for days, put on the turquoise satin dress and the white gabardine cape she'd sewn herself from a Vogue pattern. She slipped on a pair of snakeskin sandals, dropped her keys into a satin clutch bag, and went to the theater with a woman friend. She returned late that evening with a Playbill and a matchbook from a place called the 21 Club. Her shoes were worn from walking for hours, but there was no disguising the unrelenting gleam in her eyes.

She brought Claudia a present, a jewelry box with a ballerina who danced in front of a mirror and behind a glass when you opened it, and Claudia imagined herself at the theater with her mother, handing money over at the ticket booth and holding the small tickets with a row letter, a seat number, and the name of the play splashed across the front.

It finally happened, not on a weekday evening because of school but on a Saturday afternoon. Mom took her to a matinee, and it was all she'd imagined it to be. The velvet seats folded up so they could pass by and back down so they could sit high up, many rows from the stage. The orchestra rose up out of a pit. Astonished, she squeezed her mother's hand. And she did so again when the conductor extended his arms as if opening his heart to her. His baton hovered. Women in glittering black dresses and men in starched tuxedos sucked in breath. The whole world stilled.

Music then burst from musicians engaged in perfect posture, bows chasing strings and fingers feathering piano keys. The swell of sound made Claudia's young eyes well up, each note and chord another dormant emotion stirred—this one soothing, that one sad; another provoking. Caught inside the swell of voices rushing her from a painted stage, Claudia turned giddy. None of this felt real, and yet it was the most real thing in the world.

Unfolding was the story of a young woman in London who sold flowers, whose coarse speech stole the attention of a bespectacled, hard-tasking man. Later, he brought her to a ball wearing her dress of shimmering satin and hair studded with jewels, and she delighted all in attendance with her mastery of the English language. Claudia's heartbeat came fast. She thought about her own and her mother's struggle to learn English in the early days and the joyful accomplishment that steadily came. This young English woman on the stage, her cockney accent gone but her heart still tethered to her heritage, stirred up righteousness in Claudia. With each song and new stage set, from drawing rooms to ballrooms to dark alleys and crowded city streets, characters showed her something she hadn't seen before. Doors opened, light and air rushed in. She was more than the frightened girl who blushed bright red when she had to say her very foreign-sounding last name in front of the classroom. Something was ready to burst from inside her too. Words. Possibility. Potential. Freedom to leave, to take flight on an airplane, and to journey to a wildly different and exotic place, like the places she'd read about in books.

AFTER THAT ONE TIME, her mother only went to the theater in the evenings on her own or with friends because her supervisor required that she work on Saturdays. Turning the key on the music box to make the dancer twirl soon made Claudia despondent. Only one more time, she asked. One more night at the theater. And she would make it last as long as she could. She took to rubbing her cheek against the silk sleeve of her mother's jacket, and the pulsing sensation would return of the theater lights turning off, the curtain rising, a new world bursting forth. There, she'd been part of a bigger whole. Not now. Not ever again. She taped the tickets inside her diary, but she buried the music box under a pile of sheets in the linen closet. No one ever asked about it.

Theater took over her mother's life. Movies did too. So much so, she quit her job at the factory and patrolled Fifth

Avenue for days looking for a new *métier*. She'd had enough of drab factory walls and sooty streets. She'd had enough of unfaithful men, too. She was determined to recreate for herself and for her daughter a facsimile of the lives she saw on stage and on screen. So, she stared into the windows and walked the aisles of Bonwit's and Bergdorf's and Da Pinna. She blessed herself with holy water inside St. Patrick's Cathedral and bought wide-brimmed *Breakfast at Tiffany's* hats. On a whim, she rented skates and twirled quite capably under the statue of Prometheus in Rockefeller Center. She photographed the mannequins inside the Saks windows and drew sketches at home so she could copy the styles she could not afford to buy. Her mother was a walker and a wanderer. It was how she made her discoveries and solved her problems. Fifth Avenue was her mecca, and one day along her usual pilgrimage, she came to an abrupt stop before a bold red door. Bold red was her favorite color, a hue so sizzling and provocative her husband said she shouldn't wear it. How delicious, the idea of scandal.

A tall mustached man in a military-style coat and with cheeks as red as Hawaiian Punch bowed and opened the transformative red door. She, an immigrant and a factory worker, had never had a door opened for her. But she recognized the name Elizabeth Arden emblazoned at the entrance. That woman, herself an immigrant, had started her business with little more than the chutzpah, or the desperation Claudia's mother felt now. She went inside as if she too were a member of the carriage trade, strutting her snakeskin heels across those marble floors.

She took the first job they offered and crossed into a new life. She wrapped fat red ribbons around glossy white boxes for the Christmas season. She altered fine designer wear sold in the boutique and worn by the salon clientele. She moved up the ranks to coat check attendant and presented cotton robes she'd ironed and folded to perfection to movie stars and foreign dignitaries. She wore the red door pin on her lapel like a military medal. She was in the battle to win it.

As for Claudia's father, he did not contest his wife's newest mandate. They were moving to Manhattan, into a fourth-floor walkup on the Upper West Side on a side street from which they could see the park and not far from the skating rink where the benches reminded Claudia of the scene with Jennifer Jones and Joseph Cotton in *A Portrait of Jenny*. Perhaps it was there, while they were lacing up their skates, that her mother told her about Caffè Florian in Venice. It was a place of embellishment and mystery. Her parents had been there once in late fall, when they were still enamored of one another and the musicians seemed to play just for them. Now, the hot chocolate her father brought them after skating was at best, according to her mother, just mediocre.

Mama's stories were intriguing and cautionary, but her father's were real and tangible. Her mother insisted on intellectual or industrious pursuits—reading, art museums, balancing the checkbook—but her father emphasized amusement. He taught Claudia to catch a softball on the fly and lob back tennis balls. Meanwhile her mother's feet kept moving: to work, around the house sewing curtains and clothing, rolling out fresh pasta, tending plants and flowers. And always back to the theater.

THE DOURNESS OF MATERNAL LESSONS, however, did not inspire careful listening, so Claudia was destined to do the things her mother warned against. The repercussions were not dire until Venice. It wasn't her fault, Claudia later argued. It was advertising. Advertising brought her to Venice the first time—not pictures of waiters swirling trays in sunny piazzas, but her copywriting job. They paid her to stay at the Cipriani, where Giulio was the sales manager. He took her to dinner so she could sample wines she would later describe as sultry or velvet laced or ripe with tannins. She could do that better than anyone, better than her mother could, because her mother had worked with her hands not her head, and a copywriting job was the mark of a girl who got through college with honors and without a single marriage proposal. She hadn't been in love with Giulio, but he was a charmer, and rules, well, sometimes it was appetizing to ignore them. After Chiara was born, Claudia made the obligatory phone call. She said she expected nothing from him, and his tone voiced relief.

Every day of the week Claudia took a ferry from her flat in Jersey City to her cubicle in New York City where she wrote slogans to lure people to buy things. *Wear your dreams like a necklace*, she wrote as she twisted her client's long chiffon scarf, speckled with rhinestones, around her neck. *Never let him lust for someone else*, she penned, and swiveled up the rose-scented lipstick. Sometimes the words flowed, whether from an internal muse or the mind-lulling effects of a late-night drink. Other times she downed multiple cups of coffee, turned herself upside down into a yoga headstand for twenty minutes, and cursed at the Hudson River, just to get a word, a sentence on the page. There was the occasional one-night stand she never felt good about but considered her only option for intimacy. Was it Hemingway who said all you could hope for in a day was to write just one perfect sentence? Well, she had many wasted days.

She told Chiara about Giulio over a birthday cake with six

candles and glasses of lemonade. All plans were in place. She was pitching a travel company to write their copy for a client trip to the Venice Biennale the following year, so this was a good opportunity to do some sleuthing and embellish her credentials without having to pay for a hotel room. Giulio reserved a complimentary suite for them at the Cipriani, where he'd recently been promoted to director of sales.

"It would be cool to meet him, Mama."

Claudia suddenly vacillated. "I want to make sure I can take the time off."

Chiara's lightness frightened her.

"Aren't you a bit nervous about meeting your father?" She stood up abruptly so Chiara wouldn't see her face flush on that improbable last word. Why hadn't it turned out differently? It always worked out for the divas of Italian film. Gina rode behind Rock Hudson on a motorcycle around the cliffs of Positano. Sofia rejected Cary Grant in favor of her true love, the dumpy Carlo Ponti. Even droopy-eyed Anna Magnani, vilified by Rossellini in *Roma città aperta* had hundreds of roses tossed over her coffin by resolute fans outside Santa Maria sopra Minerva in Rome.

"Nope! I have to tell Abigail. Is he a prince or something? A magistrate?"

"You have no idea what a magistrate is."

"Sounds cool, though."

The hotel's private water taxi bounced over waves toward the leafy island of Giudecca. Cold canal water sprayed over its sides. Claudia drew a jet-lagged Chiara close and leaned back into the mist. As the boat gradually approached, she felt every part of herself unravel like the coiled rope the captain now handled. The monochromatic emptiness of water and sky bled into a Turner palette of gray, speckles of morning sunlight on water, the distant palazzi-like dots of history in repose. Gardens, lots of gardens hiding things. The bunkers of Venice, she thought wickedly, taking out her pen and notebook. The motor went mute, and the boat bobbed gently, lulling its two tired travelers to nap.

Minutes later. A thud. The hull hit the pier. Mother and daughter opened their eyes. The captain reached out his arm to help them out, but Chiara had already leapt ahead. She raced down the driftwood walkway into a labyrinthine garden swallowing her up like Alice in Wonderland. Claudia followed, past shriveled rose bushes that still held their summer scent, past terra-cotta pots of russet and gold chrysanthemums.

Inside their suite was a fruit basket on a table and a small gift wrapped in lavender tissue on a windowsill. Compliments of the Cipriani. She lifted open the window and wrinkled her nose at the canal stench. Decades of over-tourism. There was a time when the air smelled of sea and stone, when one could dock alongside the forgotten islands of Venice and climb out of an old wooden *topa* to wander amidst the ruins of grand palaces covered by brambles, the stones of a past when the city felt wide and golden and lush with mercantile promise.

Such idealizations existed only in cinematic colorations now.

Chiara raced in and bounced up and down on the mattress, squealing. An unsettling sensation took over Claudia as her daughter leaped, toppled down, and leaped again, higher each time. Children were so agile, but not forever.

Time to get to work. Shower first. Words. Words needed space to form their illusions. Claudia undressed and stepped into a tall rectangle of marble. She pumped lilac-scented wash into her palms and lathered up. What themes could she play and play off of here? Venice was music and mystery and seduction. The conquests of Casanova, the bad-assery of Peggy Guggenheim. Sunshine and stench, gondolas like coffins, musical notes at the helm. Venice wasn't even a real city. It was a cluster of islands on the water, a floating menagerie in the spirit of Narnia or Atlantis, untethered from social constructs elsewhere. Take the Biennale. Copy could spin: *After perusing bold and brilliant artworks designed to transform your perspectives on humanity, morality, and social responsibility, summon up the wildest degenerate art muse and take your greatest risk.*

She heard Chiara squeal excitedly. Claudia turned off the tap. Perhaps for her parents, Venice signified a beginning and an end. The beginning of innocent passion and the inevitable slow death of everything.

Seriously, Claudia. You do know how to be a downer.

Dried and dressed, Claudia was being hugged by Chiara now. They always felt so free when they traveled together. Pieces of obligations peeled away so they could hug and inquire and chat.

Herbal tea arrived from room service and spoiled the innocence. A note from Giulio. She rehearsed in her mind:

"Chiara, this is Giulio, your father. Giulio, this is Chiara, your daughter."

This was a mistake. Retracing the steps of a previous mistake made only a mess.

Chiara was simply staring out the window, however, at the boats charging past, leaving triangular wakes: the *vaporetto*, the yacht, the smaller private taxis. Resting her elbows on the windowsill, she started to hum.

GIULIO KISSED THEIR HANDS, led them to their dinner table where white linens glowed under crystal chandeliers and a harpist played against the solemn backdrop of the moonlit canal. He pulled out Chiara's chair first, whispered in her ear that she was beautiful. She shrugged off the compliment, but her eyes fixed on him as he flicked open his napkin and placed it ceremoniously on his lap. He pulled at his white shirt cuffs, and the glitter of a jeweled cufflink caught the light.

Chiara looked down at her place setting, then at her mother, and lightly tapped the appetizer fork. Claudia nodded. What she wanted to say was: Why do you care?

Giulio told one story after another. Naturally, he was the hero in all of them. He spun his own analyses of challenges, accomplishments, of people who expected less of him and were surprised of his brilliance, of terrible hurdles that, in effect, were not unsurmountable. He'd excelled at Boccone, Milan's premier business school, and earned one promotion after the other while working in Venice's most illustrious hotels, the Danieli and the Pitti Palace.

The names meant nothing to Chiara, even as he filled and refilled her glass with sparkling water and told her repeatedly how pretty she was. Of course, the compliment was for himself. His genes in full glorious display. He was even more effusive as she took the right knife and fork and to cut away at her carpaccio with the flair of a Venetian socialite, rolling her eyes or looking away to find a distraction. Claudia wanted to kick Giulio under the table but saw his eyes soften as he watched his daughter drink from her glass. So, she withdrew her foot.

She knew she would never trust him, or any other man of

his age, to be alone with her daughter. Why was her mind going there? Giulio was not her own father. He had, as far as she knew, always been transparent and fair minded. Chiara had some of that quality. What you saw, you got. Claudia watched their eyes, father and daughter. Both pairs as blue and transparent as the Murano water pitcher at their table, in a secret dialogue she was excluded from. Giulio rubbed the girl's cheek and squeezed her hand. What right had he? Her hand tightened into a fist under the table. Chiara and Giulio liked each other.

"So, Chiaretta, what do you want to bring home with you?"

Giulio gestured for the waiter to bring over a tray of pastries.

Chiara would not be distracted.

"A glass bird, with wings up," she said, before pointing to a chocolate millefeuille. "*Questo qui,*" she told the server.

"They make glass birds in Murano, but the wings are flat."

"I don't want one, then."

"Why not? They're still very pretty."

"I don't care." She dug her fork into the creamy layers.

"Of course, if you want something special," Claudia said, "I'm sure one of the many glassmakers here can make one for you."

For the first time that evening, Giulio looked uncomfortable.

He was less uncomfortable, later that night, when he showed them the penthouse, a glass-enclosed suite, dark except for the flicker of votives and lights from boats sailing up the canal. He poured Claudia a glass of champagne and more sparkling water in a crystal flute for Chiara. This was his home turf for the week. A sales conference hosting a hundred employees of a software firm in Milan required he reside at the hotel until the attendees left. His actual home, where he lived with his wife, Raffaella, a prominent pediatrician, was in Mestre, a suburb a long land bridge away.

"This reminds me of home," said Chiara, drawing her knees up against her chest on the sofa.

"Jersey City isn't Venice, darling."

"Well, Mama, we do have to cross the Hudson to go to work and to school." She looked at Giulio. "We live in New Jersey, but we go to New York every day on a ferry that takes only seven minutes to cross."

"That seems very quick and very efficient. I admire Americans for that. I would like to come to New Jersey one day to see your life there, Chiara. You can show me New York, too. We can take bicycles around Central Park."

"Oh, yes. And we can kayak on the Hudson River, too."

"We will plan on it, then." He handed over a dish with three chocolate truffles. "Please enjoy these. I need to speak with your mother in private."

And so it happened, as she feared it would. The conversation in a sitting room with a screen separating them from *their* daughter, who at the same moment was savoring truffles and thinking about a brave new world unraveling in front of her and the presence of a father rediscovered.

"Claudia, I know you don't want this, but I can help."

"It's not necessary."

"Very little in life is necessary. But it doesn't mean we don't crave things. Much of what gives us joy is unnecessary, but the soul needs nourishment, it needs connections, moments like this. And you've kept me away long enough."

"You're saying this because of where you are right now. Your son is grown up, Raffy's success and independence threaten you, and squiring a child around New York will make you feel young and relevant again."

She intended to hurt him. She didn't like high-minded gestures covering up for self-interest. Even worse, she was feeling the attraction again, the sense of freedom and unbridled pleasure from that one time.

"Now that I've met Chiara, you can't keep us apart forever. I am still her father."

"With what responsibilities? Tell me? What role can you fill for her given your situation and mine? You have your own family. She is my family. Just the two of us. Do you realize how confusing it would be for a child her age to—"

"She doesn't seem confused to me."

"My answer is no, Giulio."

SHE STARED at the departing *vaporetti* the next morning, over a cup of tea in her own suite, as Chiara dressed in the bathroom so she could make faces in the full-length mirror behind the door. Whiffs of Chanel No. 5 filled the room.

"Not too much, Chiara!" No more spritzes, but a lively humming flowed from the room as the girl found another distraction. Claudia opened the window, fantasizing about that first early-morning ride across the canal, the most exhilarating moment of each visit. Act two of the *commedia* was about to start and she had no idea how it would turn out. Movies again. *Summertime* with Rossano Brazzi. A flirtation with a handsome stranger at a café table in San Marco. Katherine Hepburn, in a red taffeta dress and glossy black pumps. An Alitalia poster caption, or a full-fledged article in the *Times* travel section. Perhaps she could pitch it as a reality show. *Best places to have illicit sex in Venice. How to tell your illegitimate child about your Italian lover.*

CHIARA SAT in the front of the water taxi, but when icy water sprayed over the sides, she stood up alongside her mother and grabbed her hand. Claudia felt a surge of relief. Her child was a child again. To assuage her guilt, she wiped Chiara's damp face with the edge of her scarf, just as the boat plunged around the long promontory of land that hid the piazza from view. And it appeared all at once, in the distance, unraveling like a ribbon separating water and sky.

Claudia saw the lady in the turban on the low bridge minutes before they passed under it. A sunbeam pushed through clouds, pierced the dark water below in green glassy swirls. The lady shouted to them to duck, the bridge is too low. The driver shouted, more ferociously than the woman. It won't touch me, Claudia decided. A flutter of dust struck her forehead. She ducked.

"Whoa, Mama. You almost lost your head!"

Brick and stone gave way to open water and sky. Claudia swung around to look behind them. The lady in the turban was resting her chin on her hand.

"Where are we going, Mama?"

Silence.

"Mama!"

"To Caffè Florian." The bridge and the woman grew smaller. Claudia felt a small tinge of panic.

"Why? What's there?"

The woman was gone.

"Mama, you haven't answered me."

"I'm sorry, darling. Pastries and hot chocolate."

"Oh, nothing special." A pout and then: "Look!"

The Campanile shot up in front of them under a bluer sky. The basilica and its gilded onion dome sprawled glamorously across the piazza, La Serenissima's prescient host welcoming the curious, the entrepreneurial, the dreamers, those seeking refuge, some from oppressive regimes, others from haunted pasts. The golden reliquary's Byzantine windows, mosaics, and stone medallions spoke of a theater of Jerusalem, Constantinople, Rome all wrapped up into one. Its articulations melding Islamic, Christian, Middle Eastern. The small actors moving across its stage are each curious transients at this once-historic crossroad of east and west, seeking beauty, answers, and perhaps a way forward along their life's journey. Venice was never simple, but for Chiara, Claudia had to make it appear to be so.

"Ahh, there's the Bridge of Sighs. Do you remember why it's called that?"

"Yes, Mama." Chiara heaved a sigh of her own and turned back to the charging boat traffic.

"Why can't we take one of those boats, Mama? We can go way over there to those other islands. That would be so cool!"

Yes, there were parts they could explore today, islands to discover, but she hadn't the energy or the will. Last night had drained her.

Artists rested canvases all along the steps of the crowded, sighing bridge. Chiara, always drawn to snow scenes, selected an amateurish *acquerello* of Santa Maria della Salute in winter. They'd just passed the church, but Claudia hadn't pointed it out. She'd been thinking about the woman on the bridge.

"Questo qui," Chiara said to the artist, her Italian as precise as the part in her hair. Claudia shrugged at the price, even though the gratuitous image of a gondolier in a striped shirt standing inside a gondola made her wish she'd honored her daughter's request to zip across the canal in one of the mahogany speedboats to less conventional locales.

The artist wrapped the uninspiring watercolor in tissue. Chiara grabbed it and ran down the marble steps of the bridge and under arches that rimmed the square. Claudia caught up, and hand in hand, they walk shadowy, vaulted corridors toward Caffè Florian.

A burnished yellow light glowed behind the stained glass. She pulled the brass handle of the mahogany door and stepped into a place of past lives. She'd come here as a student, a tourist, a business traveler. She'd written copy at the corner table and sketched a layout for her apartment renovations. She'd had an evening aperitif here with Giulio, when she'd played at being someone other than who she was. Travel allowed one a certain role switching.

This time she'd come on a different mission, but was she playing someone she was, or someone she wasn't?

"Near the window, Chiara."

Chiara ran to the green settee. A pink marble table with sturdy iron legs stood proudly before it. As they slid into the settee's velvet cushions, their backs to the veined vintage mirrors, a spicy-sweet tobacco scent spiraled over, like smoke from Aladdin's lamp. A silky voice lured Claudia to look across the room, and she was not at all surprised to see the lady in the turban.

Her voice suited her. It slid and shimmered like the

taffeta shawl around her shoulders. It pirouetted like the amber gold light in her eyes. But there was, yet, a contradictory raspy quality to it. Gold bands encircled the index and ring fingers of both her hands, studded with rubies, tanzanite, and amethyst. Wisps of blond hair framed a cherubic face. Tiny lines etched her mouth and framed perfect white teeth. Movie star teeth. She could have been sixty or seventy, twenty-five or a hundred years old. She held up her cognac glass.

"Davide."

"*Subito!*" The server took the glass and stepped behind the bar. Behind him woodcuts of Venice lined up beside photographs of film celebrities and the occasional oil painting. Claudia took out her notebook to jot down what she saw.

"Is that an *acquerello?*"

Claudia, startled, turned. Chiara had unwrapped her acquisition and held it up for the turbaned woman to see.

"Ah, Santa Maria della Salute."

The wide, button eyes wouldn't let her turn away. Chiara ran to the woman's table, holding up the awful *acquerello*. Claudia didn't move. Where had she seen this bizarre and beautiful face before? Why did its expression hold her so firmly in place?

Because she had been in front of this woman before, Claudia realized. She had seen this face up close. It had haunted her since a Sunday afternoon when she and her mother arrived late to the movie theater and had to sit in the front row. As the projector rolled, her mother whispered every tragic line of *La Strada*.

Nine-year-old Claudia had cried when the trusting and funny Gelsomina curled up on a cold street and shivered to her death alongside that brute Zampone, who only then, through uncontrollable tears, realized how lonely he would be without the sweet little clown before him.

The eyes held her still, once again. The eyes of a disillusioned wanderer, of a prosperous matron transformed into a scintillating diva, of a simple candid soul so firmly rooted in hope that when the ultimate misfortunes fall on her she needs only to see a group of schoolchildren to smile again. She was the ever-hopeful Cabiria of dusty streets and devious men and the proud Signora Boldrini of the Roman upper classes in her villa in Fregenae. She was childlike mischief and female sexual power. She was vulnerable, and she was strong, and she held out her hand.

Claudia realized she'd crossed the room and was standing in front of her.

"I am Giulietta," she said so with surprising humility.

"I know."

"Please join me." She gestured for Claudia to sit beside her.

"How do you know her, Mama?"

Claudia swallowed. "This is Giulietta Masina, Chiara, a very wonderful and very famous Italian actress."

Chiara's eyes opened very wide. "You're an actress?"

"Yes."

"I'm Chiara."

"A gorgeous name. Odd for an American."

"I know." She raised her chin. "My mother's name is Claudia."

"Ah, like the actress Claudia Cardinale. I know her well."

Chiara's eyes open wide. "You know other actresses?"

"Lots of them. But then we're all actresses of one sort or another." She looked again from mother to child. "I imagine you are an actress, too, sometimes."

"Yes, I want to be Amanda Seyfried. My friend Abigail says I look like her. Mama thinks so, too."

Giulietta pushed aside her empty cognac glass and the ashtray. "We have a saying here in Italy. *Meglio solo che mal accompagnato.* Better alone than in bad company. I hope you'll consider me good company." She snapped her fingers at Davide, who was carrying a tray of miniature pastries. He brought it over.

Chiara pondered tiny chocolate éclairs, *mille foglie,* and *sfogliatelle* curving like seashells.

"Choose the ones you like, Chiara."

"But I like lots of them!"

"So, take lots!"

"Only two, Chiara."

Chiara frowned and picked up an éclair and a *mille foglie.* She looked longingly at the chocolate chip-studded ricotta cream nestled inside its cannoli bed. Giulietta put all three on her plate. "We will make an exception today." She winked at Claudia.

Chiara thanked her and popped the super-gifted *sfogliatelle* in her mouth. She dabbed her lips with the napkin on her lap.

"This is why I come to Venice," said Giulietta. "You think you can resist temptation, but why should you? Have a pastry. Swim in the Lido. Fall in love. Dance in the street. Why not? You are not in Venice every day. You think you understand everything about life, and she shows you don't know anything because you close doors around you to make yourself safe. But you are never safe, and it's so much more fun not to be so."

Chiara looked up at her, puzzled.

"You see, Chiara, you think you can see through a person, a situation, but of course you can't. What you see is perhaps a façade, like the façade of the Gritti Palace or La Fenice, or the

Palazzo Ducale with their secrets. Even today Venice is beautiful, but she is also ugly. She is ugly in her cruelty to those who do not have the means to luxuriate in her luxury, who cannot come here to the Florian." Giulietta dabbed a tear from the corner of her eyes. "My husband makes films. He does not like Venice. He prefers Rome. He says it's honest, more carnal."

Davide placed two cups of Turkish coffee on the table. Claudia was about to object. Giulietta thanked him. "Another one of my indulgences. After you drink, I will read your future in the grains."

Claudia watched Giulietta down the sludgy brew as thick as chocolate syrup. It was far too bitter, but she drank it down anyway.

Chiara sighed and rested her head on the table but opened one eye wide to stare into the gold flecks inside a dome-shaped glass ring on Giuletta's hand. Giulietta slipped it off, held it up to the light. Chiara's eyes followed as if tethered to an invisible string luring them upward. "It's Murano. The glass is so fine, it's as if it isn't even there. Glassmaking is one of the arts of fire, Chiara. It takes a lot of heat to shape it, make it bring in the light so the gold sparkles. See?"

She tilted the ring to catch the light above them, and the sparkles did seem to catch fire.

"Oh yes! It's so beautiful!" Chiara's blue eyes shone brighter than the chandelier crystals. "Arts of fire," she repeated.

"Yes. That is their power. Heat melts resistance, the physical and the emotional kind. We need heat in life, Chiara, or we never break free and become as beautiful as this. Look at the facets and the light that this releases, the clarity, the excitement, so much happiness to grasp. Sadness, too. But even in sadness, there is life. More of it actually."

She raised her wrinkled hand higher, closer to the light, and the sparkles, no longer static, did seem to dance. Claudia remembered the ballerina inside the jewelry box she'd thrown away.

'Your mother should take you to the island where they make the glass."

"Can I get a glass bird there?"

"Of course."

"I want a flying bird, with its wings up. Not flat."

"Naturally. The others are far too boring. You should ask for what you want." She raised an eyebrow at Claudia. "You *can*, you know." She pulled a card from a silver card case. "Don't go to Murano, but to Burano. Less commercial. There is this glassmaker there. He works alone. He will make her the bird."

As she put the card case back into her purse, she glanced at her coffee cup. She furrowed her brow, tilted the tiny cup back and forth. A dark sludge formed half-moons around its sides. Behind the bar, Davide put down the glass he was polishing. *"Che c'e, Giulietta?"*

Chiara looked up at her mother, concerned.

"I see." Giulietta paused. "I need to go home. Davide. *Per piacere*, can you phone for me?"

"Subito!" He disappeared through a swinging wooden door. Voices, ruckus from a back room. Claudia imagined arms flailing and the frantic rush to a phone somewhere in a stainless-steel kitchen where counters were lined with baskets of breads and Hungarian pastries on porcelain plates. Soon the lunch dishes would come out: *salumi* and cheeses, arugula with shaved Parmigiano, and creamy pumpkin soups sprinkled with chunks of amaretti. But the mood of Caffè Florian had

shifted. The soothing gray outside the window pooled thick. Raindrops pelted the window.

Giulietta's eyes became playful again, like those of a child who had just discovered her lost marble behind a tree. And just like Cabiria. She tilted the coffee cup towards Claudia. "Amazing how something so opaque can speak with such clarity."

As if the clarity gave her the strength to do it, she stood. Davide, eyes down, kissed her hand, helped her with her shawl, and offered to escort her through the front door into the drizzle. But before leaving, she turned to Claudia. "I will not be here tomorrow. You will be, so walk everywhere. Walk all over Venice. Walk the bridges. Don't take the boats. You miss things. And you should go to the Accademia. They have a wonderful exhibit of antique crystal. It's in the Dorsoduro." She leaned over to pat Claudia hard on the back. The point was not lost on her.

Giulietta looked once more at the coffee cup on the table, her eyes filling. She closed them for a moment, then motioned for Chiara to open her hand as she dropped the domed ring into her palm. She closed the child's fingers over it and squeezed tight.

"Promise me you'll go to Burano, Chiara. It's one of Federico's favorite places. He says it's more honest than the rest of Venice."

They watched Giulietta disappear into a tangle of streets behind the piazza, a solitary orb fighting the wind from the canal. All was gray except for the purple turban and, finally, the red umbrella she popped open before picking up her pace.

～

"THE ACCADEMIA IS HERE in Dorsoduro, a name which literally means *hard backbone* because it's built on solid topsoil."

Chiara barely listened to her mother play tour guide as they wove around tiny squares and narrow alleys. They paused their rapid steps just inside Campo Santa Margherita where Algerian peddlers in long muslin robes laid out blankets to display designer knockoffs. If one were to film *La Strada* today, they would be the gypsies traveling from one village to another, and Gelsomina would be among them, folding up the blankets at the end of the day, proposing a shiny red wallet to a disheveled tourist, searching naively for someone to offer her a bit of food and an encouraging glance. The piazza sprawled around them, a circus of real life, human misery played out against a movie set of baroque palazzi, fourteenth- and fifteenth-century houses, cafés, fish stalls, and *erboristi* selling alternative medicinal cures. This beauty was the backdrop to the ugliness Giulietta spoke of, civilization after civilization. Humankind created; humanity destroyed.

Chiara bought lavender and dried chamomile. Smells from bakers' ovens drew them in for a gargantuan loaf of bread, which they devoured, picking off the sesame seeds as they did.

At a shiny new gelateria, a young woman with elaborately tattooed arms packed the top of a cone with *semifreddo.* Claudia thought she should be named Gradisca like the earthy, full-breasted temptress in *Amarcord.* But where were the frenzied pubescent boys following her with lustful shouts and grasping hands? Perhaps in a new version of *Cabiria,* the children would put down their tiny metallic cell phones to jump on the edge of a fountain and lick their gelati and *semifreddi.* One might even offer some to the devastated prostitute, who until now had believed that nothing will ever make her smile again. But something does, and she carries on. That little face brightens like the streetlights in Times Square, as impromptu as a burst of song from an opera tenor who has lost his way and knows only his voice, his talent, can ever help him find it again.

The bridges brought them here, each one loping over water to anchor onto solid land. A misty dampness settled over the square. She remembered, now, the old Venice, the city she missed, the wisteria of Venetian spring and the *acqua alta* of its silvery and mystical winters, white masks over black capes during Carnevale, and the scene of Maria Schell with Marcello Mastroianni in *Notte Bianche*, alone on a bridge. Snow falls softly around them, all is white, and the love affair that has reached its zenith falls away with the sudden appearance of her lost lover.

"This is such fun, Chiara. When you walk over the bridges, you are airborne, suspended, not quite sure and then you are grounded again on the stones of a piazza that sneaks up on you and when it opens up you have your choice of places to go."

Chiara didn't grasp her mother's lyricism, but she enjoyed the dark chocolate gelato she scooped up with a tiny spoon. Claudia watched people walk out of the antique shop with small lavender bags. Giulio probably purchased her gift there, knowing she had a penchant for antique inkwells.

"What are you thinking about, Mama?"

"Nothing, darling." Just the novel she would never write.

"Oh, yes, you are. You're spacing out, like you did on the boat today."

"You're probably right."

"And you nearly lost your head!"

She giggled and dug out one more creamy scoop. Claudia caught sight of a flutter of pigeons in a trash-filled alley and turned her eyes away. They walked over more bridges, into tunnels, along dark streets, and under shuttered windows. They walked past imposing palaces on the Grand Canal and silent neighborhoods around squares and alleys. Robert Browning had written here in the Palazzo Barbaro. Ezra Pound lived here with both his wife and his mistress. And on any given night during Carnevale, wealthy British expatriates took gondolas to neighbors' palazzi for champagne and revelry and to gossip about Peggy Guggenheim, who walked naked into the canal on the anniversary of her father's death.

Such decadence, such glory, and in the end such sadness, she thought. Because everything at some point comes to an end. Because humans make the same mistakes over and over again. We create and then we destroy. We learn our selective lessons. We retrace our steps, in the hope that somehow, someday, we will arrive at that mecca of true understanding and connection. It takes a lot of wandering to get there, and a lot of getting lost along the way.

That's why to savor the honesty when it comes to you. Discover another bridge to cross, linger a few moments in a small quiet piazza, look up at clotheslines and the people talking to their neighbors from balconies on high. Postal coach arriving via bicycle, and a young woman in bright attire carrying letters in her arms. But what about the street merchants? Where do they sleep tonight and when the colder winter comes?

She and Chiara would skip dinner with Giulio. He'd just have to understand. If he didn't, *peccato*.

∼

He was waiting for them, seated upright in a Fortuny chair, a martini beside him. He bolted up and clasped his hands.

"Have you heard? *Che tragedia!* He died today."

"Who?"

"Who? The maestro! *Fellini!*"

Now it was Claudia's turn to sink back into the chair.

"What's the matter? Mama? Who is Fellini?"

Giulio passed his hand over his eyes. "He was the greatest filmmaker of this century, Chiara. Your mother knows. We grew up with his films. Your mother on one side of the Atlantic. Me on the other. It happened just this afternoon. A heart attack in his garden in Rome. I'm sorry, Claudia, Chiara, but I can't do dinner tonight."

Claudia tried hard not to show her relief.

Upstairs she called her parents. The customary phone call to let them know all was well, so they could hear Chiara's voice. They were doting grandparents of an only grandchild. Her father had abandoned his philandering ways in the later years. Her mother had continued working, and they seemed to have grown closer as they aged. Her mother asked if she'd taken Chiara to Florian for the hot chocolate. Claudia had quite a story to tell. She gushed about Giulietta, about the exhilaration of the moment, words exchanged, eyes in conversation, the intoxicating magic of the surroundings.

As she spoke, she sensed her mother's delight. She felt the warmth of stage lights, the exhilaration of curtains and music rising. She was at the theater with her mother again. The conductor raised his baton. Music swelled in the room. Somewhere, in front of multiple mirrored reflections, her ballerina was dancing. In each panel revolved a new facet of the life to come: a cottage by the sea with a garden where Claudia could finally plant lilacs, adopt a rescue dog, maybe say yes to that cute guy's invitation to brunch. Now open Giulio's gift, dip the pen into the crystal inkwell and write, write what comes to you, write about today, write about the dancer's choreography that brought you here, this day, this moment. Don't stop. Up the tempo. Leave nothing out. Write faster. Now slow down, adjust the rhythm but keep writing. Write about what hurts and what fulfills, write about the absurdity of self-doubt, write about seeing past fear, and dancing into the fire.

A final *élevée* on that last note, arms high. The dancer will bow soon, her performance complete.

CHIARA WAS BUNDLED UP, and Claudia couldn't feel much of anything but the raw chill against her face. The water sprayed high. They were alone in the boat. A sliver of moon and quieter waters under a veil of mourning. She felt a pang of sadness as they passed under the bridge where she'd seen Giulietta in her turban.

Inside Caffè Florian, all the televisions were turned on. Waiters and patrons gathered around to listen to the commentator from RAI. Spectators sat frozen in their chairs. Many cried. Hands stroked filled glasses. Plates of food untouched.

Claudia lifted Chiara onto a barstool. Davide brought her some blood orange juice. Claudia thanked him, but her eyes remained on the screen. She played with the tassels on her purse as she listened to the broadcast.

The maestro is survived by his wife, Giulietta, and a son. Their son is flying in from Albania tonight. Giulietta was with her husband when he died. It was as he wanted. Ms. Masina, like the maestro, always had an uncanny sense of premonition. He called her to say he wasn't well and could she please come home. She took the next plane out of Venice and arrived in time. As she'd always promised, she was with him in his final moments.

And, on the screen, Claudia saw the lady who had been a diva, a waif, a prostitute, a clown—a woman who, in her lifetime, played all the roles women around the world had played over and over, for centuries, a brilliant and beautiful woman who'd been a leading lady from the day she was born. "Walk the bridges," she'd said.

THEY SAY Burano is the island where the rainbow fell. The glassmaker grabbed at the hot molten glass with steel prongs, pulled up and shaped two wings on either side of a blue bird. The mother watched, but when the sculpture cooled, he handed it straight away to the girl who stared out the window, distracted by a row of brightly colored buildings on the other side of the canal. She thanked him, slid the bird into her knapsack, and walked out purposefully, toward the small bridge that would take her to them.

THAT TIME OF DAY

Florence is waking up—or as awake as she will ever be.

Anna slung her tote over her shoulder like old times and dragged her bag down the steps of the Santa Maria Novella train station. Behind her, the gardens of the Basilica rose up as viridescent they always had, dark and teeming against the pale rose gold of the sky. Herbs and blossoms sprouted hopeful under freeform trees, continuing to project mirth and frolicsomeness down the whole length of the sobering geometric patterned stone leading to the Officina Profumo-Farmaceutica di Santa Maria Novella. There, Anna would find the patchouli oil no longer available elsewhere, thereby erasing the apprehensiveness this morning of rubbing the last remaining smidgen on her wrist when hurtling toward Florence. A whiff of the familiar in a now unfamiliar place.

But as the gardens placated her with their flaming incongruities, the streets disconcerted with their de Chirico silence. Only she and three other people crossed the intersecting cobbled streets against a pointless red traffic light. Something else she hadn't paid attention to in years past: people in tattered clothes sprawled against buildings. It was warm but an elderly man had wrapped a torn blanket around his shoulders. A shirt-less, younger one poured water over his head and shivered it off. Children slept bare-cheeked against the pavement. One woman held out her hand even though few people walked by, as if she were a phantom, or they were, or both. Everyone was afraid to handle cash or coins. Anna, too, didn't have any money on her. She had nothing to bargain away her guilt as she jerked her suitcase around and walked to the Officina, one of the world's oldest apothecaries, its eighteenth-century founders, the Dominican friars, having mixed curative balms and elixirs from the medicinal herbs in their gardens now in nearby Castello on Via della Petraia.

She brought her wrist up again to her nose. Perhaps inside the grand apothecary, she would collect, along with the patchouli oil, some fresh ideas for her business, a lifestyle boutique in Bath stocking eponymous hand-made candles and room diffusers. Before, bloggers and influencers from as far away as Pondicherry paraded her florals and resins in front of thousands upon thousands of eyes. Then the novel coronavirus stopped the pageant.

Thankfully, even after shuttering her eco-conscious shop during lockdown, her online business continued glinting promise. More people staying home meant more people surrounding themselves with soothing scents. She owed her particular success to Iride. It had been her idea to use only soy wax because it was non-toxic and cruelty free and all that stuff mattered in a world overrun by soulless consumerism. Go sustainable, she'd said right after her first chemotherapy treat-ment. It's the Italian way. Every scent has a provenance, a story tethered to nature and humanity. Your creations should be a calculated and gorgeous marriage of both.

Her mother always had a way of setting the bar high.

THIS TIME, and for the first time, Anna walked alone under the frescoed ceilings and multi-tiered chandeliers of the Officina. It wasn't simply the passing of Iride. Anna was the lone visitor. No footsteps trailed her down the mirrored hallway from Via della Scala. No whispers. No echoes. No faces passing by. The void made her own reflection disappear.

The grand salon, a fragrant and lavish chapel, had stunned her twelve-year-old eyes upon her initial visit. With its gilded arabesques, its celestial ceilings, it had looked like a step back in time. Now thirty years later, it looked like its time had passed. If she were searching for inspiration, she wasn't going to find it here. Apparently, she wasn't going to find the patchouli oil either.

"It's not possible. How is it discontinued?"

This last word sounded injudicious. One didn't discontinue Santa Maria Novella's patchouli oil any more than one would discontinue its signature potpourri made from the stems, leaves, and buds of flowers found in the Tuscan hills and which, thankfully, was still sold in a silk pouch from the Antico Setificio Fiorentino, embroidered with golden thread.

"We no longer carry the essential oils. But have you tried any of our fragrances?"

Anna, unmoved, scanned the row of bottles in front of her. Acqua di Colonia di Sicilia had been one of her mother's summertime indulgences. She'd snapped it up that bright summer day, spraying the suntanned clavicle bare above her white sundress, her red lips explosive. A lily of the valley oil rounded out her purchases. Anna had opted for the patchouli. It was bolder. Iride then decided to have her defining perfume custom made at a shop on Via delle Belle Donne, owned by Iride's close friends Gabriele and Ivana. Iride's passing two years ago had hit them and their daughter, Romina, hard.

It was long past time for a visit.

Anna checked her watch. She was to meet them at the shop at seven o'clock. They'd decided to sell after forty devoted years. Also, long overdue. Grimly, Anna contemplated skipping out by eight, evading the late-hour Italian dinner; she would take a long bath and get to sleep early enough to wake up in time for the eight AM flight out of Pisa.

She'd allotted only one day for this whirlwind trip. Florence was not where she wished to be.

"I don't wear perfume," she said curtly and paid for the potpourri.

THE HEAVY WOODEN doors to Palazzo San Niccolò were thrown open and from the portico she saw all the way past the small wine window, the lounge, and the library to the yellow light of the garden. A flowering Judas tree stood beside a familiar sun-speckled table. Iride, always prone to dark humor, blamed the betrayal of her body on the years of juice cleanses, self-care, and quiet meditations under this very tree. Anna stayed still for a full minute. She gazed up toward San Miniato on the hill, wondering if its mosaics still sparkled gold and amber. That single gesture grounded her, here, now, in this place where they'd stayed for a month, the final mother-daughter trip before Iride became too sick to travel. Their habitual haunt, Caffè Rifullo, was just up the street. Every morning they would order the cornetto with crema filling, an orange *spremuta*, a *mochaccino*, and, over fortifications, map out their day.

Her phone buzzed and up came a photo of a young woman, sunglasses in hand, eyes arrested upward, hair blowing against her face.

"*Buongiorno*, Romina."

"*Anna! Benvenuta*! Do we meet at Michele's?" That voice. The stabbing sound of youth.

"Sure. I've just arrived."

"Are you too tired?"

"Not at all. See you in an hour."

Just enough time to check into their Florentine home away from home. *Iride's* home away from home. Florence was her mother's place, a city she could never leave behind and to which her daughter had always shrugged *ho-hum*.

London was Anna's town. Everything felt solid there, in place, definable.

"*Benvenuta*, Anna. *Mi dispiace tantissimo.*"

"*Grazie*, Federico," she said, accepting the palazzo owner's condolences. His clasping of her hands startled her. No one broke pandemic protocol. That Tuscan something now nearly broke her. So few words in just the right tone. Whatever it was, it made things better. Perhaps definable didn't always cut it.

She ran up the stone staircases to their third-floor suite. Why was she suddenly so eager to get there? She pushed open the door as if expecting Iride to be inside. Instead, only the huge armoire stood sentinel, separating the sleeping area from the living area. A cone of light fell over patterned terra-cotta floors, sultry white linens brushed against the nightstand on *her* side. On it sat a tray with a pot of the palazzo's signature tea, a mix of mint and jasmine. On one side, slices of lemon, biscuits; on the other, a single linen napkin, a single white cup. An invitation to cocktails and a book reading. Federico had added, "We made some changes to the garden as your mother suggested. I hope you like them." She laughed hard, maybe for the first time in months.

She checked them out via the small spiral staircase in the sitting room, which led up to the balcony and overlooked the gardens. A peaceful but welcoming silence. It's okay to grieve. A minute to take in the scents of cypress and hibiscus, to wave to the same woman now watering her geraniums on the *terrazza* across the way. But no lingering to listen for cicadas. It was too early in the day, and she was still her mother's daughter. Time to unpack and make the foreign place an ally. Stories past. Memories preserved.

Possibilities nestled inside the folds of fabric she lifted out of her suitcase, neatly unfolding like origami. And now you consider your setting, the space you will inhabit indoors and outdoors. What you unpack, the necessities and the flourishes, are all part of the experience. How do you dress for the protagonist you are?

For today, Anna decided it would be the black linen sundress with thin straps and a tiered flouncy skirt, accessorized with Iride's "disruptive element." In this case, a studded belt to *mettre en valeur* her slender waist. The totality was a bit of mourning and a bit of Fellini irreverence. There had been no time for a pedicure. Nude flats would have to do.

She had the room flourish in her tote bag, but first she had to finish unpacking. This time Iride couldn't argue with her choices. Out came the silk shantung blazer to wear with everything, sparkling ballerinas from Milan, a skirt copied from the Patrizia Pepe boutique. Iride could copy anything, but when she could no longer sew, she found a *sarta* on Via Maggio and sent magazine clips of outfits for herself and for Anna, along with reams of fabric and measurements. Items of impeccable fit and styling, like the blue linen sheath with tiny pearl details and the sexy teal slip dress, the floaty *go big or go home* palazzo pants; these would arrive a few weeks later. She hadn't brought those. She was only here for the day. For the slim possibility of an additional one, she unpacked some pretty lingerie and a silky black sheath. She took her time unfolding the shawl from an artisan by the sea in Viareggio. One had to take care of one's things. They were not inanimate. They had a soul and a purpose. A shawl could promise warmth on a cold evening, envelop your shoulders as a lover might, and then, folded over a chair or on your bed, became part of home.

Now, the flourish. She took out her *Stai A Casa*, the Italian version of her Stay at Home candle. That one had sold out during the promotion to encourage her fellow Britons to respect the lockdown. For the Italian version, she substituted orange flowers and white musk. But it lacked something. Iride would have known what that was.

SHE SHOULD HAVE COME SOONER.

There's a new vibe in this city, her friends had said last summer when she'd canceled her trip once again. It's not Milan. And it will never be Rome, where you're always seduced to do what you would never do anywhere else. But, oh, Anna, the new boutiques and *aperitivi* bars, the carnival insanity of Pitti Uomo, the hot guys hanging out in Piazza del Carmine, that late-morning bike ride, balancing an espresso on one hand.

But Anna expected to see none of that today as she crossed

the empty Ponte alle Grazie. She clicked on her cellphone to check the temperature and to distract from the encroaching stillness.

Six months ago, before the outbreak, it would have been easier. The streets packed with tourists and the ubiquitous tee-shirt stands would have diminished the impact of what she saw —the bare bones of Florence, her buildings stripped of grandeur or intrigue. Their stories in shadows. They stood alone and disconnected, as if in judgment of the humanity that emerged ever so sparingly along her streets.

Outside Caffè Concerto Pazkowski, a man set out tables at least six feet apart. He placed a hand sanitizer on each one. Who will come? Who will stay? Who will linger over morning caffè and cornetto in quiet? Who will dare to converse with a masked stranger behind plexiglass? Will any *return?* In this place where centuries ago they all did return—the artists, the literary intelligentsia, the thinkers and scholars—to write or to talk for hours about the plight of the social classes, the evolution of governance, the inevitability of a future plague. They talked among themselves and with strangers. They drank cognac and grappa. But not now, this month, this year. So, she turned and walked back toward the river, to the stone railing that ran alongside. She leaned against it and looked down into its sluggish and murky waters.

Something about the water and the quietness. It was reminiscent of another time: her father's passing, so suddenly, a heart attack while the three of them hiked around Laguna Colorada, a crimson-hued lake in Bolivia. Her father had leaned over his walking stick to point out the red algae under the water's surface. He held up his binoculars for her to look at the pink flamingos walking along the shimmering water.

"We'll come back again," he said, "in winter when all these

jagged ice caves form around the basin and bubbles freeze under the water's surface."

And in those few moments, before it happened, she'd felt the world was perfect. He was only forty years old.

SUNDAY MORNING in Piazza della Santissima Annunziata meant the church bells rang even though the basilica remained closed. She quickened her pace, planning to run through, but as she rounded the corner, the luminous piazza snapped open in front of her like a rebuke.

It said: See, really see, the snowy white and *pietra serena* walls of the Museo degli Innocenti on the left; the Loggiato dei Serviti, their mirror image, on the right. Take in Ferdinand I galloping on horseback straight ahead to the Duomo.

Anna let the piazza's breadth fold her into the symmetry of the Museo's nine arches. It brought to mind a pop-up book her architect father had given her. She'd giggled as the cardboard arches sprang into formation and she wiggled her finger inside. *History's first blueprint,* her father had said. He instructed her to note the blue and white ceramic rondels, then the swaddled *bambini* by Andrea della Robbia. A marvel of order and clarity. And today, unexpectedly, history's blueprint of something else, something both monstrous and human.

The Museo degli Innocenti was once the Ospedale degli Innocenti, an orphanage for abandoned children who'd lost parents to the plague and to multiple wars or whose parents could not care for them. At one time the wheel, a hidden revolving door, allowed a baby to be brought to the Ospedale without the parent being seen or identified. They put their own child down, a piece of fabric often tucked inside the child's swaddling as a memento, and then push the door closed, never to see her again.

Anna held the name *innocenti* closer than she ever would the word orphan. Orphan implied a condition and no responsibility. *Innocenti* said the opposite. It said, you can't look away. It asked, what is your role here? Do something. Those of the Renaissance did not question whether or not the *innocenti* were worthy of care. On the contrary, the Florentine silk guild commissioned Filippo Brunelleschi, Italy's most revered architect, to design and to oversee, along with Leon Battista Alberti, the orphanage's construction. Abandoned children had as much right as wealthy adults to be surrounded by beauty.

Now the sight of children sleeping on the pavement outside the station was a daily event to forget. The brutal irony of the contrast, the then and the now, the humanistic Florentine ethos of a merchant class who thought a gallery of works by Botticelli and Ghirlandaio were an innocent child's right, and the latter that said tearing a child from the arms of a parent was the right of the powerful.

A text from Romina said she's running late. Anna bought her admission ticket and went inside.

AS SOON AS SHE ENTERED, the unadorned vaulted ceilings stopped time. Monochromatic walls erased assumptions. Texts and timelines pierced ignorance, unfolding stories of thousands of infants abandoned to the wheel. Plaques named each wet nurse, listing the children she cared for.

Despite so little embellishment, it made her feel so gratefully alive.

She entered another room. A single structure dominated, a

curved cabinet of sleek blond wood inset with rows of small drawers, each one marked with the name of an innocent. A young boy, perhaps eight years old, in a black tee shirt and white linen shorts, opened one drawer at a time. The presence of another live body felt surreal. Two live bodies. His mother shrugged at Anna.

"He won't leave until he's opened them all."

Anna opened one, too. And then another. And worked her way around an entire row. Inside each drawer, preserved under a square of plexiglass, were the mementos left with the children: broken medals, where the parent kept one half and the child held the other; notes of love and letters to the parents and grandparents; and shreds of fabric, photographs, drawings.

IN AN INNER COURTYARD, now empty, children once played. The surrounding cloister and porticoed archways offered shade. No one had played there for centuries, of course. Sitting down on one of the benches, she turned off her phone. Children of every century invented games and excuses to run and jump for hours. Did they Double Dutch, jumping from side to side in-between competing ropes? Did they hopscotch, hop down the squares on one foot, then two? In winter, did it snow? Was it thick enough to dig holes with frosty fingers to roll marbles into? Anna still kept a clear marble on her nightstand, next to a photograph of her parents filling clam shells for Christmas Eve dinner. Simplicity is deceptive, her father instructed. You cannot rely on embellishment or drama to distract from an unforced flaw.

Anna should look at her watch, but she didn't. She reentered the *museo* instead. From memory, she navigated through the cloister and climbed the stairs to the roof. This was ritual. In the face of beauty or its hard truths, one went to a caffè or bar and talked about it. None of that talking was available now. Because of Iride, because of this century's plague, because she was single and traveling alone. Still, she ordered an espresso.

She drank it like an Italian—one toss—and put the cup back on its small saucer. As the breeze ruffled her hair, she wondered if the Duomo was stalking her. It popped up everywhere, all the time, all those years, and now again, way off in the distance beyond the terra-cotta roofs. At the end of Via dei Servi, looking down from Fiesole, above and beyond the flowering trees in the Gherardesca gardens, at the end of another street near the Sant'Ambrogio market and Teatro del Sale, where she had gotten lost and was told by her father: Find the Duomo and she would find her way.

"ANNA!"

His voice took her by surprise. The sun blinded her on the steps of the museum. Michele's red *motorino* pulled up. There he was, wearing a mask but no helmet. Those green eyes, and those forearms, shirt sleeves rolled up. Be still my heart, she thought.

"Anna! Romina is waiting. I came to look for you."

He was right. She glanced at her watch. Two hours had passed.

"And you have Gabriele and Ivana this evening. You want your perfume, don't you?"

"Well, no, not my perfume. I don't wear perfume."

He frowned. "I can't believe it. What are you wearing now?"

"Patchouli oil."

"Really? That's all? I like it very much."

So, they were flirting a little. This was new.

"I—I asked for the formula to my mother's perfume just to keep it. Or to make a candle or a diffuser or something. To commemorate her. It would be good for my business."

God, that last line.

"But you didn't come here only for your business, Anna *cara*." Again, those eyes.

"No. No. But..." She looked away. She wanted the perfume formula so it could never be worn by anyone else. Transformed into a candle, it would remind her of home when her parents were still alive, when she still felt whole.

"I see. So, Anna! We have a lot to talk about before your meeting, you, me, and Romina. Hop on!"

As if she would or could say no.

So, they flew, or it felt like flying, like maniacs down the narrow Via dei Servi, hurtling predictably toward the luminous marbles of the Duomo.

"*Ecco*, red from Maremma, green from Prato, white from Carrara! This is the six-hundred-year anniversary!"

"Of what?"

He stopped abruptly, eyes above his mask shocked.

"Six hundred years ago Brunelleschi began construction of the Duomo! And you are a daughter of an architect."

They took off again. How he navigated the *motorino* with one hand and barely a swerve she didn't know. She held on tighter. Into the shockingly deserted Piazza della Signoria, under the shadow of an equally somber Castelvecchio. Then down Via dè Tornabuoni. All those languid afternoons strolling in and out of Cavalli, God Save the Queen, Prada, Bulgari. She straightened the red Valentino sunglasses Iride had insisted she buy, even though they cost her a week's salary and she'd just quit her job as a lawyer at Harrod's because the stress was killing her along with her failing marriage. Today they filtered the hesitation hovering in the too-still air. Fashion is both salve and spark, Iride would say.

"Palazzo Spini Feroni! You remember, no? You're wearing the Vara shoe you bought last time." He glanced down at her shoe or at her leg, hard to tell which, but he did smile. Hand up in the air again. She grimaced as he whipped around Piazza Santa Trinità, nearly slamming into the obelisk of Justice. He was cute but he was crazy. This was new, too.

"Guarda che capolavoro!" He stopped with a jolt in front of a pair of Vara bow pumps in a window, looking oh-so-sexy in red alongside the iconic rainbow platform shoe Salvatore Ferragamo designed for Judy Garland when she won the Oscar for the *Wizard of Oz.*

"Buy them!" Michele said now, pointing at the red ones. He and Romina had convinced her to buy the Vara flat she wore today, a cross between pink and beige.

"Michele, the store is closed."

"So what? You know how they fit. Order online and they will deliver to your hotel in one day. Or I will bring them to you and slip one on your foot like the prince in that silly fairytale."

"You are seriously insane."

"I hope so." He turned serious. "Anna, no more can we say we plan something tomorrow. This is the lesson of lockdown. *Maledetto!* My Zia Federica lived in Sydney. I promised to visit her so many times and each time I went somewhere else,

Bhutan mostly. She died a few weeks ago. *Tomorrow* is a word I hate."

He gripped both handlebars. "I wish I'd come to London to see Iride before she passed. And, in some ways, I will tell you later, maybe with a strong Negroni in my hand, I nearly lost myself. Buy the shoes, Anna! Your mother would already have them on her feet."

Anna tightened the arm around him. She could have said she knew about loss, but even after her loss, she wasn't sure she did. The pandemic had changed everything, including the rush to rhetoric to make one feel more comfortable, even more virtuous. Still, Federico's condolences earlier had been heartfelt.

"So?"

"So what?"

"When are you going to buy them?"

Why, oh why, couldn't she just fling her arms around his neck and kiss him right there in that triangular piazza? Because he was in love with Romina, she reminded herself, which was why the flirting earlier had startled. He had been amorous for years, despite Romina's fifteen years behind him and her preference to remain unattached.

"I'll think about it."

That stare.

"Okay, but you have to do that prince charming thing."

She could flirt, too.

"Without question."

The scent of Italian leather followed upon his statement. Because of the proximity to the shoe museum, she assumed it was tanned shoe leather. But no. It came from the watch strap around the wrist Michele waved and the surface of his tan mail carrier bag. Or was it the dry down in his cologne?

"We need to get going," she reminded him. Too much playing inside her head. Time to sit with Romina and hear about her new plans. Her parents weren't happy, but they rarely were with her choices. Until recently the plan, on their end, had been for Romina to take over the family business. Passionate arguments ensued, with both Iride and Anna taking Romina's side. Iride, who'd worked as a luxury home goods buyer for Selfridge's, had offered her a London-based trainee position. London, Paris, New York, perhaps Dubai, those were the options and opportunities for someone as fierce and as restless as the lithe young woman who biked around the city as if she owned it, aced all her exams, and declared to her sentimental father that she planned to stay single for her entire life. Motherhood did not interest her one bit. It's like dying before you're dead, she'd said the evening she, Michele, and Anna shared a joint in Piazza Tasso with two students from Senegal. Michele had turned his head before the façade of his face fell.

OF COURSE, everything was changed now. For Anna, too. A part of her that had always wanted to be a nomad, but a nomad with a home base. Now after months locked down in that home base, she thought maybe it was better to be constantly on the move.

Was it easier to be a nomad knowing you still had a family and a place to call home?

"Now that Ivana and Gabriele are selling, there's less pressure for Romina to stay here," she said to Michele in a futile attempt to break the percussive silence. He started up his *motorino* without saying a word. The smells of street dust and gravel, of leather, of the hint of citrus from his neck, all combined with something wary, wearied, beneath the austere Palazzo Spini Feroni.

A detour due to closures to traffic forced them away from the river and back onto Via dè Tornabuoni. When they passed the Palazzo Antinori, Michele stopped in front of the bar Procacci.

"Should we get a panino here?" he asked.

"Oh no! I've been dreaming about your panino for days!"

"I'm hungry now, though. Wait here. I will pick up for three."

Anna wanted to protest. But within the context of the past five months, it didn't feel right. Michele's silence confirmed a general new distaste for pretensions. A truffle panino from Procacci sufficed, even though this was not truffle season.

The few customers sat outside at tables—a spare crowd, but a lively one. Locals only. The bar stood empty. She remained on the *motorino*, waiting for Michele, missing the old days of sipping Aperol at the bar with her mother, and the way Iride would repeatedly squeeze her hand when they argued. Even with no one waiting for her in Bath, she wondered how soon she could leave.

He returned, canvas bag over his shoulder. "I scored us our favorites. For you, *un panino prosciutto e crema di carciofi!*"

"Thank you." She blinked back the renegade tears and pressed her fists together. Now she really wanted to kiss him.

"For me *panino salame e burro di tartufo*. Even out of season, the burro is, is, how you say?" He kissed his fingers. "Ama-a-zing! And for Romina, who is the most brave and wants *everything* on her panino..."

He waited for Anna to fill in the blanks.

"Mortadella al tartufo con crema di tartufo e funghi."

He gave her a thumbs up. It took the edge off his abrupt-ness earlier and they were off again.

Without explanation, he took a longer route touring some of her favorite streets.

They crossed the Ponte Santa Trinità into Oltrarno; they coursed down Via Santo Spirito to Piazza del Carmine and beyond. Here and there, bars set out tables for *spuntini* and wine. A few boutiques and the print shop offered glimmers of contemporary flare. Sparsely populated streets remained all the same.

"Your *gelateria!*" They passed the gleaming doors, but oh-so-dark now, on Ponte alla Carraia and then flew down along the Arno to cross Ponte Santa Trinità again. There, although she wished he hadn't, he chose to stop.

"She loved it here," he said, after a brief silence.

"Especially at dusk. She liked the colors of the sky."

"*It's at dusk that all the flowers release their final burst of scent before closing their petals for the night,*" he recited.

"It's her. Every word. Exactly what she said every time!"

And it was all happening again. The light was just begin-ning to soften and descend. In a few hours, the sky would become a watercolor of lavender, rose, and amber brushstrokes, until it lowered and embraced them inside its dome, the *insieme* of the city.

The citrus of his cologne was starting to dissipate. Some-thing warmer emerged, mixed with cypress from the hills beyond. Like the clearing water of Venice, the clearing air filled Florence. She closed her eyes, seeking the emergence of jasmine, the sensual flower of promise, according to her mother. But it was too early in the day.

Few people crossed the bridge they next raced over. Some dangled legs over the stone ledge, gelati in hand. Some guided children; others, elderly parents. Her mother had moved like that, slowly first with the cane, then with a walker, and when she could no longer walk, she just wanted to die.

Anna tightened her arms around Michele's waist and hid her face in his shoulder.

IF SHE'D EXPECTED exhilaration upon arriving at Michele's caffè-bar on the corner of Via delle Belle Donne, the past couple of hours had prepared her. Outside the windows, empty of movement, stood six tables for four under white umbrellas. A few locals took espresso or a *granita di limone*. Boxed flowers hemmed them in from the street. The blooms were exotic, artfully layered and vibrantly colored, of species and variants she couldn't name but would swear suggested Romina's hand. That meant they would be undoubtedly local and sustainably grown, employing fair trade principles. And there she was, Romina in all her outrageous glory, leaning against the entrance, arms folded. This creature of art and flowers and wanderlust wore wooden sunglasses made by a craftswoman who was part of FAF, Female Artisans of Florence Collective. Romina had told Anna as much on a video-call months back as she recounted one of her last finds before the plague shut down the shops. Next to her was Alba, the proprietor of the lingerie shop next door. The bar, just like at Procacci, stood empty beyond the door. Empty, too, were the shelves behind the large Marzocco espresso machine. The mirrored back wall, again like Procacci, had fewer liqueurs out. The glass case for Michele's famous panini was gone. The mahogany base still gleamed from years of care. The espresso smell was as sweet as ever, but Anna was struck by the sobriety of what had been the liveliest venue on the street, in all of Florence. Always full of chatter, sometimes song, Michele running inside and leaping over the counter to get to his machines for *caffè, spremuta, granita*. His was the energy that made Florence less sleepy to her.

Those hours of the past sank inside her so deeply. They marked the start of her current life. She'd composed her first candle here, not at home, strategizing *en committee* with Romina, Michele, Gabriele, Ivana, and of course Iride as creative director. Anna left Florence with calm, purpose, and a business plan, while Iride remained behind to go sailing with a mysterious friend in Sardegna. Some people needed meditation. Others, adventures on boats. Anna just needed Michele's bar.

Romina hugged her, violating the covid code. Her long, floaty caftan billowed around her. Anna recognized it from Instagram. Romina got it from Adriana, an Italian now living in West Harlem who sourced many of her fabrics from Africa.

When Anna complimented her style, Romina twirled around. "We start to wear the world." This was a new look for her. "I'm leaving Florence very soon. So much to tell you!" This time she hugged Anna harder, drawing quick quizzical looks from the sidewalk collective.

Michele called out to Piero, his second in command, to disinfect a table and to bring out water and some plates. "Anna is a special guest," he announced as he pulled out a chair with a flourish. "Make sure to give her whatever she wants—if we have it!" He winked, squeezed her hand and he was off to make them all Negronis.

Romina sat across from her and lowered her mask. She was gorgeous, as always. But this time, her dark eyes gave off a radiance at once startling and composed. As Italian as she was,

Romina could have been from anywhere, while Michele remained essentially Florentine despite his world travels. Romina evinced a global force. No one country or continent could claim her.

"I can't believe you are here!" She clasped Anna's hands. "With a new business and a new life! And me too! Next week I go to Zimbabwe."

"Really? For how long?"

"For good. I will come back to visit, of course, but I am so happy for what is happening. It is a boarding school for girls. They are building it because the girls are alone in the day when their parents travel to South Africa to work. They are not safe. I learned from a visitor in my parents' shop that there is a women's group in New York partnering with an NGO. I saw a video of a girl. It changed my life. I sent my bio and my letter of intent, and they accepted me!"

"With your taste and style, you will design a beautiful school."

She frowned. "Anna, at first I was thinking about color and cotton linens and planting flowers, and we asked the girls what was important for them." She paused. "Only shocking things. Barbed wire and a female guard."

Of course, when basic safety is denied you, all else falls away.

"Then soap, and clean water, and female hygiene supplies."

Anna nodded. Even during lockdown, she'd had access to all her essentials, including scented soaps she took so much time selecting in boutiques on her posh street. She'd never felt unsafe, not a day in her life.

Michele came out with a tiered cocktail plate of olives, peanuts, buttery parmigiana chunks, and a large white straw hat. He put it on her head.

"What are you doing?"

"It's still hot under the sun. And you look *très* Audrey Hepburn."

She tilted the brim and touched the black grosgrain ribbon around the crown. It coordinated well with her black dress. Iride not only would have approved, she suspected this was her hat.

"She bought it before our first sailing trip to Sardegna."

So, this was what he needed the Negroni for.

"*You* were her mysterious travel companion."

He patted his chest.

"Guilty. Me and Isabella. You remember Isabella. She owns the boat, so it was always the three of us, talking, sailing, swimming, drinking."

This unsettled her. It was also wicked fun.

"And what did you talk about?"

He shrugged in his matter-of-fact way. "Everything. Your mother, as you know, had many interests."

She stared him down. "And some secrets."

Romina left the table to show Piero how to mix an Aperol for the Swedes at the next table.

"We talked a lot about you, Anna, especially the last time. She wanted you to have the hat and for Gabriele to make a perfume for you. She said it is time for you to give up only patchouli and to move on. So, after you left to return to Bath, she and Gabriele and Romina and Ivana and I, the committee, came up with a composition. It is almost complete."

"You got together to create a perfume for me?" Silence. Those eyes. Deep breath. "Without my input?" He nodded. "Okay, committee, why isn't it complete or finished?"

"Because *you* need to finish it, Anna."

Of course. Damn him. The committee. Them both.

"Were you sleeping with my mother?"

"Perhaps." Another matter-of-fact shrug. "You will never know. I will never tell. If I did, I don't regret it, and if I didn't, I do. And it doesn't matter. She loved you very much. We spent most of our time together talking about you. I got to know and love you more through her words. And then more by creating your composition, telling its story of you. That's all I will say. Do with it what you will."

Her mouth must have fallen open because Romina giggled as she returned to their table with a small vial, a handful of scent strips, and a notebook. "I was the creative director for this project, Anna, so I hope you approve."

She sparkled now more than ever, humbling Anna to silence—and to watch, transfixed. Romina slid the scent strip into the vial and brought it slowly to her own nose. Anna didn't reach for the strip, but the notes danced across the table, uninterrupted. First, a surprising mix of marine notes and basil, then green notes, neon florals, and leather. Anna closed her eyes. Michele's mail carrier bag, his watch strap, her mother's suitcase, all from the same artisan, a truth revealed. Patchouli was barely present but there as if to give her a foothold, like the stirrup she slid her riding boot into that winter evening years ago, hoisting herself up so she could ride for hours along the windblown beaches of Cornwall and forget how much she'd wanted her marriage to end.

Anna already knew the scent before Romina passed over the bit of paper laden with flowers, resins, memories.

"It opens with marine notes, ozonic, fresh like the sea, because that is the note of possibility, of going to a new place and setting yourself free. Remember that time we all went to Sardegna but you couldn't come? We were going to meet Isabella in Cagliari to sail for seven days. You had to return to

Harrod's for a conference, but we missed you and talked about you at night over glasses of *mirtillo*. It was only Michele, Iride, and I. My parents had to remain here with the shop, but they promised to stay in touch with you and to make sure you got home safely."

"Yes, they were generous to check in on me." That was only partially true. At the time, she thought it intrusive and was frustrated that her mother once again extended a trip that was too long to begin with. But, of course, they all knew there was no conference. She was returning home to confront Brad, to tell him she knew he'd cheated on her and to send him away, to clear out every last vestige of him, his books, his clothes, his cologne, his bicycle, which she threw down the stairs and into the trash. Only a few days later, she put the apartment on the market.

"The middle notes are hibiscus and cypress and a bit of geranium because of the garden in Palazzo San Niccolò, where you stayed with your mother. She said you did yoga there. Restored yourself there."

She did. She would roll out her mat on the marble tiles that had once been a dance floor. Then lay out her blanket, her blocks, sprigs of lavender. The pungent scent of jasmine rolled in with the evening, coasting on soft music from the library, her amber and vanilla candle flickering in the sultry darkness, the promise of sliding into linen sheets as crisp as singing cicadas.

"She was hoping you might one day like to travel to India to study yoga more seriously like she did."

Not a chance. Third-world countries were for romantics like her mother and adventurers like Romina and Michele. Anna needed her comforts.

Romina, once more, read her mind.

"We thought at first to include white and purple irises because it is your mother's flower and the flower of Florence, but we decided against it."

Somewhere in Anna, resistance sprung to attention. She'd longed to visit with Iride the south of France, or New York City, or Bolivia again—but with her mother it was only Florence. Even so, the perfume pushed its way into her, *her* perfume, battling the resentment until it retreated. She gasped.

She had caught it now.

A novel and unexpected patchouli note ushered in a flawless transition between the scent's heart and its soul, but it did not resemble any patchouli she'd ever known. This was a composition in motion. It was on the move. It would not stay still. It would not be defined or contained. And this time it did not stand alone. A sizzling floral, herbaceous accord matched it, a burst of verbena and balsamic needles, heralding a bustier embroidered with Bulgarian rose and jasmine, all wrapped in a leather jacket with pockets full of sexy sandalwood.

Anna wanted to be this woman, wearing the bustier and the leather jacket, the woman who entered a room enveloped in this scent. It was glorious. It was fearless. It burnished the hidden facets of herself, the broken pieces, the works in progress, the doubts, the silliness, the mistakes.

What is it like for others to write your life's story, to carve out your past, and direct you toward your future, without prescription?

"Look, Anna."

Her Negroni glass was empty, and a full one had taken its place. Michele pointed to the sky.

"Il Duomo!" said Romina.

"*Hai ragione! Andiamo,* Anna!" Michele cheered. "We must go there now. It is the six-hundred-year anniversary.

Filippo would want us to celebrate. Finish your drink first! *Dai, forza!*"

Anna started laughing.

"I feel like a college freshman at a pub on King's Row!"

"Yes, but at the pub you don't get Michele's Negroni. You get only cheap beer."

"Hey, there's a lot to be said about a Guinness on tap."

So that she wouldn't get too drunk, Michele did what good Italians always do. He gave her more to eat. Elena from the *fiaschetteria* across the street brought over a *schiacchiata al olio*, the classic Tuscan flatbread brushed with local olive oil and, in this case, topped with a few cherry tomatoes.

"Take your time, Anna. Do not hurry," said Romina. Michele held up his hands in surrender. "The sky will change slowly. And the Duomo, after six hundred years, is not going away. We want to be there at just that moment when the light is everything."

From behind them came the familiar voices of two co-conspirators.

"*Ma guarda che cielo!*" Ivana, a paisley shawl around her shoulders, hair entirely gray now, reached her free hand at the sky and directed her bicycle competently with the other. Gabriele, plumper than Anna remembered, in his haphazardly buttoned cardigan, swung the shiny Profumeria del Sogno shopping bag, clipped shut with a gold foil seal. Iride's perfume. Anna laughed, at the sudden absurd realization that her mother's life was there, encapsulated in a few vials and a notebook to be set on the caffè table in her favorite city in the world, in front of her committee as if she were still holding court.

"I think we will go to the Duomo together," said Gabriele.

"Now, Anna, what do you think of our composition—for you, I mean, not Iride. Hers is complete. Yours..."

"Mine is lacking. Is that the word?"

"A bit strong. But yes. I think empty." He had a habit of wagging his finger for emphasis.

"Well, I'm not feeling empty now, given everything I've eaten."

"Good! Then you have the *forza* to come with us to the Duomo!" Ivana made a fist. "And then we will tour the wine windows because this is history too, *cara!*"

For the first time, Anna sees the ever-chic Ivana as less embellished but more fulfilled. Gabriele, still an avid runner, sported his pandemic pounds without apology.

In true Florentine spirit, they knew nothing was assured. Their history taught them plagues spare no one. Michele, she realized, looking back at the empty bar with fewer bottles and no panini, assessed his losses with cautious but regenerative curiosity. And then there was Romina. Romina's life would never be empty. Not even barbed wire would hem her in—not, too, the young women she would protect.

They knew the future is hard won. Florence taught them this also. Their city led the world out of the dark ages into a renaissance of innovation, humanistic thought, and artistic splendor. Under the sky's chiaroscuro light and the burnished stone of their Duomo, its people were prepared to usher in a new, more youthful, more diverse, less predictable, and more infinitely modern rebirth.

They locked arms and walked, sometimes in single file, as they funneled along the star of streets across Piazza della Repubblica, around the turning carousel, to Santa Maria del Fiore and Brunelleschi's crowning masterpiece, Florence's heart center.

Beneath their feet, the wide *pietra serena* stone plaited strength and solidarity in a herringbone pattern. The four Florentines and one Englishwoman laughed, chatted, and strategically avoided the wine windows as they moved along with the crowd.

"Without plagues, we wouldn't have the wine windows. We wouldn't have the Duomo either," said Romina.

"We wouldn't have had *this* Duomo, the most magnificent in the world." Ivana corrected her. "Your father told you the history, Anna, I'm sure. The Cathedral of Santa Maria del Fiore was built over 150 years. In 1334, Giotto designed the bell tower. Then everything stopped, first because of wars, then the black plague. As a result of so many years in between, the octagonal walls to hold the dome were expanded, posing an almost impossible challenge. How to build the cupola, unprecedented in scale, requiring an entire forest of scaffolding."

"It was a puzzle only Brunelleschi could solve," chimed in Anna, echoing her father.

"When Michelangelo climbed up into the Duomo so many years after, because he had been commissioned to build the dome of San Pietro, he said, 'I can build a larger dome, but never one this beautiful,'" recounted Romina wistfully, taking Anna by surprise.

They greeted friends among the socially distanced crowd. Anna had been just a girl when Cristina, the *farmacista*, had offered her lavender soaps and scented toilet water, when she'd fallen off her bicycle in front of Gianni's print shop—and then those significant few years older when she'd had her first kiss with a guard on top of the stairs inside Palazzo Strozzi. This evening, each of those faces appeared in the crowd of Florentines threading their way to the Duomo, the masks unable to dim the unique life force of each.

She walked to the rhythm of conversations. Brow lines deepened on faces she'd known for decades. Smaller and younger eyes turned upwards, racing past her, the offspring of people she now remembered. New faces, too, graced the *pietra serena* stage, a full global palette of artisans who'd flocked to Florence from Asia, Africa, and South America to study with its masters of leather making, fashion, jewelry, winemaking, and the culinary arts. Once again, Florentines old and new would join together and lead their city into a modern rebirth, as yet undefined, and in many ways terrifying, but with the explosiveness of the previously unimaginable being made into physical forms.

An arm slipped around her. Romina. Next, a hand slipped into hers—Ivana's. Anna squeezed Ivana's fingers and touched Romina's hand with her own. Gabriele hovered just over her shoulder, close, like a sage, quiet Renaissance angel. She didn't know how long she'd been crying but her face was wet.

And where had Michele gone? Anna looked around.

There, a short distance to the right, framed by Ghiberti's Baptistery doors, Michele strode toward them. The glint in his eyes needed no mask-less face to reveal his satisfied grin. From the crook of a finger swung a rectangular bag, one that was *Wizard of Oz* red, tied with a white bow. A bag from Ferragamo.

Once again, a whiff of leather from his watch strap passed over her as the bag passed from his hand to hers, different somehow from the scent she'd picked up hours before. This scent paused midair before blending with the white pachouli and herb-tinged jasmine from her wrist, as if moving into a seductive and changeable dance. Tango, to be exact.

"Michele, you are incorrigible." She hoped her face didn't give away too much.

"As if you didn't already know that."

Behind her the air shifted, a space opening around the two of them, their three companions stepping away.

"So, Anna! Gabriele, Romina, and I will go on. The wine windows are calling us. We will see you tomorrow morning at Caffè Rifullo for breakfast at nine o'clock sharp?"

"Yes," she said, looking at Michele.

She couldn't say goodbye to any of them now.

"If we get there early, we will save your *cornetto alla crema,* okay?" said Gabriele.

"And a *marocchino,* only with shaved chocolate," added Romina, twirling around in her caftan.

Ivana got on her bicycle and pointed up at the Duomo. She winked at Anna. Around and above the cupola, brushstrokes of lavender, amber, and gold mixed with a renegade whiff of cypress—a celestial nod to her. The Duomo *had* been stalking her for decades, everywhere, across oceans too, and now it had placed itself, where it had always intended, in the center of her world forever. Even a flight back to London wouldn't change that.

ANNA UNLOCKED the door to Palazzo San Niccolò. Her heart pulsed at the click of metal against weathered wood. She took a deep breath and rested her forehead against the door, just for a second, happy to be there.

She pushed the door open. She and Michele walked down the floor-lit hallway, past the library, and up the stone steps into the amber-hued garden. A full moon cast light through the trees over the marble dance floor like a disco ball in full twirl.

What inspired them to dance could have been anything,

the music across the street, the new red Vara shoes on her feet, a soft drizzle dampening earth and tree bark, cicadas in full chorus now, her own hand brushing against the stone of a sealed-off wine window before Michele took a hold of it.

Or it could have been the unequivocal note of promise. Another jasmine, this one night-blooming, in that moment and at her own time of day, would round out her composition. She was ready to choreograph her own dance steps in the perfect shoes. She couldn't wait.

GREEN APPLES

Timothy likes only green apples. The red ones, he says, have no taste. During the kindergarten year, he told me not to squirt the slices with lemon since they don't brown as quickly as the red ones. So, I packed them in his lunchbox every day beside a sandwich of tuna in olive oil. Never with mayonnaise. Sometimes I put in a cookie, and there was always a bottle of water.

Green apples are so sour they make me scrunch up my face, but I keep eating because there's a crisp, delayed sweetness when you get close to the core. Tim says, That's nonsense, Mom. But, then, he's always had a higher tolerance for sour.

Three days before my first green-apple meltdown, my father goes into the hospital. Rectal bleeding. Serious, but not so serious he can't walk into the ambulance on his own. That is the last day he walks. And even though he's gone in for something that doesn't seem life-threatening, I know he isn't coming home. After so many trips to the hospital, there is always the one that does you in.

When I arrive at the hospital, he's ranting. My mother has

to fix his pillow. She has to straighten the blanket she's folded so stupidly. She has to take his notebook out of her purse so he can write something down. She has to trip the attendant to get yet another pillow, and she has to help him off the gurney so he can go to the bathroom. That's when I step in.

For the past year, he'd call me out of the blue with an eclectic mix of questions: Who wrote *Crime and Punishment?* What was the name of the Italian mouse on Ed Sullivan? What was Roger Maris's batting average? He would call my son on that one. Often, too often, I would slam down the phone. I was waiting for Tim to call and tell me he was on his way home from school. Sometimes he called, mostly he didn't. When he didn't, I imagined the worst. I imagined all the risky things he, in fact, ended up doing. But I wanted to believe that he wouldn't take a subway to the South Bronx to sleep with his dealer. His phone call would reassure me. All I needed was a ring and his voice. All I needed was the lie. But each ring was my father calling back. Sometimes I struggled to give him a response. Yes, I remember when Princess Grace married Prince Rainier. And that music at her funeral? You've asked me a thousand times. Yes, it makes me cry to this day. Samuel Barber's "Adagio for Strings." Yes, you're right, he'd tell me, and I could imagine his eyes filling, as if this were the ultimate gift doled out, a validation from his oldest child at this precise moment. It was all he needed to smile. Just one answer a day. Sometimes, I gave it. Other times, like the time Tim didn't call and came home from school after six, or the time Tim did come home but with self-inflicted bruises snaked up his arms, I just slammed down the phone. But my father would call back. He would call other people. He'd write notes in his book.

Still in the emergency room, I now throw out questions, and not surprisingly, he answers each one, and better than I could have. We invent our own Memory challenges. I'm bored and I need to keep him from harassing everyone. So, I dig into the recesses of my own declining memory as he bats out: What did Walter Cronkite say at the end of every newscast? What were the names of the four sisters in *Little Women*? Yes, I remember when you gave me the book. I was seven. The sack of Rome, what was the year? What year did the *SS Andrea Doria* sink? Who was the mysterious lady in black who would put flowers every year on Valentino's grave? Do you remember the words to *Cavalleria Rusticana*? I'll sing them for you. And he sings, finger tapping against the air. Everyone's looking at us, Papa. What do I care? Finger swirls up and out. He's conducting the Vienna Philharmonic. You know, Mascagni based the opera on a short story by Giovanni Verga. Do you know that Mozart never made a single correction on any manuscript?

How did we go from Mascagni to Verga to Mozart, Papa?

He shrugs. It's all art, *cara*. Comes from here. He pats his heart, the site of all his joys and all his multiple illnesses, and I smile.

It's after midnight. The orderlies are still promising an actual sleeping room, but ten hours later, my father's losing patience. He kicks around. He wants to leave. I wonder if he's afraid he'll die there. I've read that people get premonitions just before they die. They see things the rest of us are spared from.

An hour later, interns wheel in a frail woman who shivers from a high fever and humbly asks for a blanket. They promise her one, but it never comes. My mother yanks one from the only empty gurney and wraps it around the woman. The woman still shakes. Thank you, she says. But she doesn't complain. My sister and I, meanwhile, badger the staff in ugly ways. We get a room at around two AM.

When I arrive home, my husband's asleep. The dogs are curled up in their beds. I change into my pajamas, stumble toward the bathroom. I rinse off my face only to discover no towel on the rod. Tottering to the linen closet, I pass Timothy's room. I usually don't look in, but this time I do.

And I notice something strange about the lump in his bed. His arm doesn't rest on his pillow. The lump is long and solid. No differentiation where his shoulders dip to his waist. So, I go inside. I press. The pillows shift. An empty pill bottle falls to the floor. I dial 911.

He needs to go to rehab as soon as possible, said his physician. Tim wants to die. It's apparent. Last night he almost overdosed. He sneaks out to meet a man. He has sex with him. The man gives him tainted pills. Tim thinks this is all he deserves from life. He's ashamed of who he is.

Which is why he doesn't defend himself when he comes home. I remind him of the rules; like my father, he doesn't care.

I don't go to the hospital the next day, or the day after, even though I have a long list of questions. I fold up the list, slip it into my wallet. I add to it during the days that pass. My sister goes to the hospital in my place. Dad leaves his own questions on my answering machine. He's relentless, even from a hospital bed. What is the brand name of that Arborio rice we made risotto that one time with? It was in your new apartment, he says, when you were first married and had no money for air conditioners. You and I stirred the risotto on the stove for twenty minutes, and the sweat was pouring off us. We drank chilled rosé wine just to cool off. When have you known me to drink anything other than red wine? But it was just too hot.

I turn off the answering machine, sit back in the sofa, and close my eyes.

Some of my questions are funny. How many hours did we

wait outside Macy's to watch the Thanksgiving Day parade? Back then, Papa, I had no idea. I didn't mind the freezing temperatures, the two-hour wait at the garage, or the bumper-to-bumper traffic on the way home. If I tell him this tonight, he'll laugh.

I've prepared questions about Italian prime ministers: Andreotti, Moro, Berlusconi. They were all useless, he will say. It never mattered what party was in power. The Communists, the Christian Democrats; it's always the same. To make his point, he'll share anecdotes about Italy after the war.

At home, Tim has packed the bags and books he will take to rehab. He's cleaned his room, watered his plants. You can't force me to go, he says, unconvinced, as he pets Bowie and Jimi. He puts on his coat, takes his gloves, throws his house keys against the wall.

My husband wraps his arm around his shoulder as we cross the front yard and bring him to the car. Tim holds onto his father's hand. He knows there is love there. But parental acquiescence is not enough. Not in his world. Not in the now. He stares out the car window as we drive away. His eyes fill as he waves to a neighbor walking his dogs across the street.

We sign him in, say our goodbyes. He hugs us both very hard. An attendant gently escorts him from the room. We stand, hands clasped, gazes trained on his back, at the birthmark on the nape of his neck. I would kiss it when he was a baby and he'd giggle. He walks away and doesn't look back. He knows he needs to do this now or he'll die.

That night, and for many nights, Bowie and Jimi curl up outside his bedroom door.

The next morning, I go to see my father. Where is Timothy? he asks. Timothy would help him pick herbs and tomatoes from his garden when he could no longer bend at the knees.

He and Tim watched cooking shows together. So, we do that now and vow to gather every Sunday from that day forward to cook or to watch someone cook. Make sure to invite Timothy, he tells me, reading my sadness with his big warm eyes.

We quiz each other on Ed Sullivan show guests. His hands swell from being poked by too many needles; his face grows pale. He doesn't want to eat; he doesn't scream for contraband flasks of wine and containers of pasta.

We joke together. We watch sunrises and sunsets. We talk about his war years and past loves, about Puccini and old friends, about the music that stirred him and the cities he will never forget. All day long, we play. I have my father all to myself, and I make up for all the answers he asked for and never got from me.

When he falls asleep, Mom and I leave the hospital to buy groceries. I don't pay attention to what she purchases. Later I will remember bunches of broccoli rabe and zucchini, the pork sausages and dried lentils, my father's favorite semolina pastas, the olive oil he drizzled on his morning bread, the sweet grape onions he chopped up for bruschetta on toasted crostini.

Weeks later, she'll say, All that food. Who will eat it now?

But, today, the thickness of lettuces and the sales on apples distract her. She shoves a bag of $1.99 green apples under my nose and orders me to buy it. I lose it. I yank the bag from her and fling it back into the bin. Leave me alone. I don't need all those apples. They'll all go to waste. With everything going on, I don't have the time to bake those apple tarts everyone wants for every family holiday, and Tim isn't around to help with the pâte brisée. Suddenly needing to breathe, I run out. I reach the car, grab the handle, and stand there, my forehead pressed against the hood. I hear my cell phone. It has to be Dad calling about something. I don't open it.

I need to go to see my son, alone. It's a marvel I arrive where I intend. The recovery center is a labyrinth of modern buildings set inside a vast woodland. I enter the first building I see. Somber adults gather around a conference table. The alcohol rehab group. I weave my way around their chairs. No one notices. Tired eyes stare at playing cards in limp hands.

My son thinks it's cool that movie stars come here for rehab. He thinks it's cool *he's* in rehab. He stares out the window as I tell him about his grandfather. So, he's going to die, he says, voice trembling, and watches a deer leap across the grass. And I won't stay.

I want to ask, Where will you run? But I do not. I ask if he remembers the time we went to Italy for my parents' fiftieth wedding anniversary. My father bought him a leather jacket and the sunglasses he wears all the time. He shakes his head. And Forte dei Marmi? Do you remember how we would walk the beach at night, and we found the cat you wanted to bring home? We even had a name for him.

You can't keep me here, Mom. I hate you.

And how about the soccer match? When Italy beat Germany, that same year we were in Rome. Your *nonno* was so happy, he drank himself into a stupor with a bottle of grappa.

I can out-drink him, Mom.

Come on, you never drank wine at the dinner table. You said you hated it.

That was a lie.

My heart races. Just about now the phone should ring. My father should be asking: What was Napoleon's favorite flower? I want to quiz him: Anna Magnani and Roberto Rossellini? Rossellini so hated Magnani, he killed her off in one of the early scenes in *Roma città aperta*. My father liked to imitate her ranting on the set.

Tim frowns. What are you smiling at, Mom?

The phone in Tim's room doesn't ring. My cell doesn't ring either. I pull into the garage, park in my usual spot, and I freeze. The attendant wants to open the door. I shake my head. The tears spill for what feels like hours.

When I enter the apartment, I check the light on the answering machine. It's still.

They gave him the wrong medication, a sleeping pill that made it hard for him to breathe. Just give me permission to put him on life support, the P.A. asks. I defer to my sister. The next time I see him he's attached to a respirator. His hands are even more swollen from blood tests; he beseeches me to let him go. We do one day, as we gather around him and toast his passing with a bottle of Brunello and his favorite aria from *La Traviata*.

Do you know that every year, to this day, there's a Granny Smith Festival in New South Wales?

Timothy sighs. He wants to hang up. I read him the description.

"Granny smith apples are light green in color. They are crisp, juicy, tart apples, which are excellent for eating raw and for cooking, but mostly eating raw. They have a harder texture than other apples, and they don't brown as quickly as other varieties."

Hah! he says. Told ya!

What famous rock group adopted the granny smith as its symbol? I need to go, Mom. Have a substance abuse group in ten minutes. The Beatles. Fine. What apple was the granny smith seedling from? Are you kidding me? This is so lame. The crab apple from Tasmania. Great. Gotta go.

I always knew when my father thought the world was collapsing around him. During the Cuban missile crisis, he made gnocchi. After Kennedy died, he taught me to make béchamel. During the Florida election fiasco in 2000, he had me come over so we could pick every single sprig of basil in his garden to make pesto. When his mother had a stroke, he made so much filling for Italian ricotta cake we could have opened a bakery.

Maybe that's why every weekend during the two hundred and fifty-three weeks Timothy spent in rehab, boarding school, and his first year of college, I would bake.

You put too much sugar this time, Mom.

Five long years have passed, and this is the first time he's come home. His boyfriend Carl is gentle, patient. He strokes their cat. My son is doing better. I say, It's the sweetness at the core of the apple. He shakes his head. Maybe I've grown accustomed to the sour.

Tim swallows a bite of the apple tart, puts down his fork. I used five tablespoons, like the recipe said. You never followed the recipe before, Mom, and you always only used four. Because you would use the French butter, which was sweeter. So, you didn't need the extra tablespoon.

I shrug. I've never been accurate with ingredients. My mother never measured anything, and I'm fine with guessing. Tim and I found the apple tart recipe in a French cookbook. It seemed doable. Once you made the pâte brisée, the rest was easy. Slices of peeled green—and only green—apples, dots of butter, sugar. Rolling out the dough was the hard part, getting it to just the right texture in between intermittent dustings of flour. If the dough's too dry, you add water; too loose, flour. You keep doing this until it rolls out without sticking. Then you pull it up, slide it onto the tart pan and press it in. When I start to crimp the edges with my finger, Tim stops me. There's an easier way, Mom. He takes the rolling pin and rolls it over the pan rim.

Crimped in two seconds.

Perfect. By the way, let's do a square tart pan next time. I saw it on *Iron Chef*. Really cool looking.

SNAPSHOTS

Roberto would have bought the lemons himself. He called them bergamot, like the fat ones we found that day at the market in Corfu. He'd press and smell their skin. He'd wrap his hand around one in a fist as if it were a talisman and slide it into his pocket.

And he walked backwards along the shore, where the waves came up over our bare feet sinking into sand. His long hair blew in the *meltemi* winds as he pointed to white-washed buildings and sun-bruised bougainvillea. I looked only as far as the curve of muscle through his linen shirt. He was healthy then, and I was filled with misplaced desire.

I don't go to the market now, thirty years after Corfu. Thirty years after Roberto stared a virus in the face and, only then, succumbed to it. I, on the other hand, order my groceries. I stay indoors. This century's virus has made me so weak, I have difficulty climbing the stairs to my bedroom. I venture outside for a labored daily walk to my Brooklyn garden plot to water plants, prune flowers, and clip an herb to zest an otherwise vapid existence.

It's not that I don't dream of covid-free forays ahead: a return to theater and museums, a summer of carefree bike rides. It's that my mental footsteps are walking me back. I miss Roberto more now. Grief has its way. It takes a sojourn and then speaks—above the din of voices from multiple screens. We didn't have them back then. Grief reminds me of when we walked the uphill trails of the Cinque Terre a year after Corfu. I hear his voice, as clear as on that day:

"Don't be afraid. You will not go far if you fall."

AND I'M THERE AGAIN on that morning.

I don't fall, but I grab hold of a jutting rock to keep myself from slipping. Below, a tangle of narrow paths wraps around a mountain sloping down into the sea.

Roberto snaps my picture. The sun has warmed his skin to a dark cinnamon color. He looks healthier than he is, especially in those serious hiking boots.

"You see what I say about the Cinque Terre? Is easy but not so much. Is not so dangerous. Don't be so afraid you miss what is around you."

He points across the mountain slope toward an old woman limping along one of the steeper paths. Her feet are steady. She rests a basket of lemons against her hip. Whenever she starts to slip, she presses down on her downhill foot, regains her balance, and continues.

I lift a sweaty hand from the rock.

"Roberto, this is scarier than you said it would be."

He sweeps his arm toward the sea. *Look out, not down.*

"Is the Cinque Terre," he repeats. "Beautiful, this land, but give many surprises."

As I accept his arm for support, I remember when he was stronger. He won't tell me this is hard for him.

"Are you sure you can do this? It's so hot and we have a long way to go."

"I can finish." He sits down and leans his head against the bark of an olive tree whose branches had withered. He closes his eyes.

I sit next to him and look around the terrain. We are approaching Monterosso, the first town in the Cinque Terre, one of five villages built into hillside terraces along Italy's Ligurian coast. Roberto is right about this land. It is both treacherous and indulgent. While its jagged cliffs and serpentine paths suggest caution, its vineyards and lemon groves invite risk so to take in its beauty.

"So, I can't convince you to stay in Monterosso tonight and spend tomorrow by the pool?"

I want a Campari and lemon twist and my bare legs tanning in the sun. For day, the new paisley bikini and silk pareo bought in Milan. For evening, a white backless sundress. I imagine Roberto's admiring eyes, hot as the sun.

"No." He sits up. "If you go to the pool, you miss this!" He sweeps his thin arm in the air again, holding his fingertips together, as if they hold a paintbrush.

The hot sun burns the back of my neck. My head throbs. I've never hiked on trails like this. I don't hike much at all.

But I promised Roberto I'd record this journey for him. I made the promise last year on the beach in Corfu, when he was walking backwards in front of me all along the shoreline, his then thick hair blowing around him.

As he closes his eyes, head back against the tree, I remove the camera from his hand to take his picture.

The Cinque Terre is, as its name implies, five lands, five

terroirs dotted up and down a rugged coastline of inlets and cliffs. On the covers of travel magazines, the pastel villages look inviting and tranquil. In life, we were being teased by the gods: Savor these treacherous turns to the sea. Savor the battered sunset. All will be short-lived. Shorter for Roberto; short for me too.

No matter how long we live, it's never enough.

In the viewfinder, his shrinking body grows distended. The eyes sink further into his head. From the edge of the frame, a misty light infiltrates, making distances unclear, including the distance between him and me.

In the end, the camera will do the work it needs to do. I shoot. Its eye will draw in what wasn't evident, something I don't see: the variations of gold veining oddly shaped rock formations, the depth of color in the petals of a burnt-tip orchid, the abundance of butterflies, a tree branch scrolling free like a Japanese etching, a veil of melancholy over a brilliant sky, and the sneaky revelations in Roberto's face. Here, he doesn't have to be honest with me. The setting is honest enough. Words become superfluous as we stand on sloping land. Our feet holding us there as if it were the safest, most natural stance in the world. How do images sneak into a photographer's eye?

ROBERTO STARTS to stir and open his eyes. I put the camera down. He pours me a third glass of Vernaccia, Cinque Terre's white wine. I look down at the sea from the cool stone bench, the sun heating my arms. I am less afraid of falling now.

Roberto points to the walls of Monterosso.

"Where every building is painted a passionate color: pink, coral, yellow. And the path is stone, so is easy to walk."

"Why did you stay away for so long?" I wonder why I haven't asked him this before.

He lights a cigarette, leans back, perhaps relieved he can finally tell me.

"I was young when I go to Milan and to France to work. I come to New York, and I am always busy, always doing chic things. No time. No real life. I see that now."

I don't respond. What he says doesn't register. No matter. I just want to listen to his voice because soon a day will come when I won't be able to.

"My home, Vernazza, is the second village. There. You can see now, far away."

This time I do look through the scuffed-up binoculars he hands me. I want to see what he sees, not what I do. I stare across the terraced landscape and imagine the much-photographed town: its seaside *piazzetta,* boats lolling in shimmering blue harbor waters—but all I discern through the haze of far distance is the church of Santa Margherita di Antiochia. How did he see this as a boy? As a young man making the choice to leave? To seek another life, away from pirates and fishermen? Away from delicious *trenette* with pesto? Away from such intoxicating beauty?

A few beats and it is I who breaks the silence.

"What's it like?"

"Vernazza is—how you say?—not spoiled. Natural. The streets are so small the tour buses cannot get inside." He pats my knee, laughs. "And, for you, is a good place for vacation. You cannot work. Impossible to check your inboxes."

"Not good. When will it be possible?"

"In Milan, before you fly home. Not before."

He doesn't say before *we* fly home.

I get nervous. I distract myself with thoughts about everything I need to do for the autumn press presentations, but my attention is wrested back. With a Swiss Army knife, he slices a peach and drops a few slices into his wine. How thin his fingers have become.

"You know, Lindsey, I have fewer choices, but I make better choices now." We fall silent.

After a moment, he sticks the knife into one of the wine-soaked peaches and hands it to me.

I bite. The sweetness is cut by acid and minerals.

"Maybe you will not miss the business side of your job," I gave him. Meaningless conversation. "All the backbiting, the politics."

"I will not miss many things for very long."

He waves the knife in the air.

"Do you remember how we talk that when I am forty, I will have plastic surgery?"

I nod.

"Now, I wish I could have time to grow old. No plastic surgery. The knife is for cutting only peaches and cheese."

THE WAITRESS ARRIVES with a bowl of fish stew. Parsley leaves float in swirls of tomato and olive oil. I break off a large piece of bread and dunk it. Below me, the waves break over rocks.

Roberto twirls his last forkful of *trenette*. "In Cinque Terre, you have the best pesto in the world." He swipes bread all over the plate. "I eat everything because now," he pats his stomach, "I don't put on weight."

He takes a sip from his wine glass, seeing how long my response would take. Eventually he gives up.

"Lindsey, do you remember Siena?"

I see the waitress watching. She is looking at this man who is not well. She is probably wondering why he is hiking, or maybe she isn't. She studies the connection between us, nods at me. Whatever it is, it means that one day soon I will be alive and he will not. The landscape around me is lovely but harsh and truer than I could ever be.

"How could I forget Siena?"

Five years ago. It was the night we almost slept together. The second time I said no. My idealistic friend, too kind, too "woke" in those days of lucrative pursuits. We'd never been right for each other, I argued, to myself, to the mirror, to my therapist.

"Our best presentation together, *salute!*" He touches my wine glass with his. It had been a success, within the context of my priorities at the time.

"Please, Lindsey." He loves to say my name. I like the way he says it. "Take my picture so you can remember me in Monterosso."

I raise the camera and bring his face into focus. I see him clearly, but my hand shakes.

In Siena, Roberto presented his newest fragrance to the Italian press. He hadn't believed in it. Once the composition was out of his hands, it became a product, tested on animals, embellished in magazines, and sold at a glass counter by a young woman or a young man who barely earned a living wage and shared an apartment with four others to afford rent. Roberto was an idealist, an actor, an aspiring playwright, an advocate for homeless youth. He'd almost become homeless once, he told me without sharing any details, and I never asked.

When he spoke, Roberto's stories reached for the history, the emotions swirling inside the people behind the supply chain. Many did not look beyond the glorious glass bottle or gilt-edged packaging, but even so, dogged idealism and visceral connection informed his creations. A fragrance was inanimate, he said, until the perfumer infused it with the darker caverns of our dreams and our fears. A fragrance should contain this weight, this heft—the materiality of our shadow selves. A gravitas or *tristezza* that fulfilled more than simple brightness ever could. While it should never enter a room before its wearer, the perfume should linger after he or she leaves, much like the wake of a ship, the fierce undulating waves revealing and burying secrets. Roberto's creations were unisex. He had no patience even then with gender identity. This creation, the one he spoke about now, could be worn by a woman trekking up Mt. Kilimanjaro and a man slipping on a pair of silk stockings. Or in reverse, or in addition to.

For Roberto, pathos made us more alive. He was always someone to venture into the dark. A misfit inside a world of embellishment and obfuscation. Me, on the other hand—I looked for sunshine to blinker the dark edges, to cast myself the perky team player. In business, it paid off to be so.

You don't understand how the system works, I'd argued with him, and he'd look past me at a spot on the wall, knowing I would never arrive at his way of thinking. Once, he flipped open his sketch pad and drew three concentric circles. Inside the smallest one in the center, he drew a heart. Inside the second, he drew a question mark. Inside the widest circle, he drew a stick figure walking. Next to it he wrote *action*.

"You see, Lindsey," he said, "you feel in your heart what

you want to do, what you really want to do." He tapped the heart drawing in the innermost circle.

"Now your mind interferes," he continues, his finger returning to the question mark. "It starts to tell you maybe yes, maybe no. You think what other people will think, what can go wrong, what if I fail." He put the tip of his pencil on the heart and drew a swift straight line across the other two circles.

"To live a real life, you need to be like this line, straight from your heart into the world. Or." And he drew a second line, which veered right in the mind circle and then left in the action circle. "If not, you come out broken. You are not honest. You are not really alive."

He made everything seem so easy. This created the spark that made every moment we spent together electric.

And he made it all look easy now as he spoke in Siena about the shawl he wove for me on a loom in his backyard in Bed-Stuy. It was one of his on-the-side passion projects, but it was grist for the commercial products he would create in order to earn a living. I marveled then, as I do now, at how he found ways to instill art and humanity into even the most material endeavors. I wondered what drove him.

Today I struggle with knowing I was one of those reasons.

He told the audience the shawl was for a lover, a friend, a mentor. It could have been for a historic figure, an admired author, a revered perfumer, or a child in whom one recognizes, with a jolt, the wisdom of an unfettered mind. He told them how the act of weaving the shawl, surrounded by flowers in his garden, became source material for his fragrance. As I handed out the scent strips and he spoke, I felt the connections take hold with everyone in the room. Before I knew it, he was wrapping it up.

"Here in this dry down all the notes: the dampened soil

and tree bark, a touch of musk, and the surprise of dark chocolate weave together like the threads in a woman's shawl. Perfume travels from your mind to your heart and finally to your soul, where all you have felt and learned, been passionate about, laughed about, cried about, feared, lusted for, converges in that final moment of rapture. The more forbidden, the truer it is."

There was silence. Applause. Then he introduced me, and I froze.

But when I stepped up to the podium, he walked to the front of the room and drew open the drapes. Exhilarated faces before me drank in their new freedom. Outside the sun was just starting to set. As I began to speak, I saw the bowl of lemons. Without touching one, I felt it inside my hand. I ruminated on the blue and white ceramic bowl, the colors of Greece, and our clasped hands in darkness rushed back to me, a sense that the world could not touch us. We were confident, beautiful, and invincible. *Tutto andrà bene*—all will go well, as the Italians say. In my mind I heard Roberto whisper, and I stifled a laugh.

MONTHS LATER, we walked along that beach in Corfu and talked about captured moments and lost moments. Could we have carved out a life together as lovers? If we had, could I, Lindsey, have saved his life? It falls into that canister of regrets. Today people claim you should write what you're grateful for on bits of paper and put them in a jar. I started such a jar, but each folded paper was a regret. Not loving Roberto was the biggest one. Not loving anyone that ferociously.

Later that evening in my room, he gave me the star-shaped filigreed pendant I still wear.

"It's for you, Lindsey, for every presentation from today on. So you will not be nervous. Is *buona fortuna.*"

He pointed to the window. It was dark, except for a few stars.

"To be worried, to be afraid is a waste of time. Look outside. You do not have this in New York. And when you are there, you don't look. Enjoy it now."

The memory of Siena flashes away, like a snapshot of Roberto when he was well.

WE FINISH our espresso and tie up our hiking boots. Across from us, on the beach, a few bathers lie across the rocks, their bodies absorbing the scorching sun. At one time, we were as they are, dreaming of nothing more than an evening strolling across the town piazza, stylishly attired, reflections of our newly tanned selves refracted in storefront windows. I look at my watch. It's almost three o'clock.

"Now, we will climb there. Vernazza is on the other side. First, we sleep a little." Roberto rests his head on his palm to show me what he meant. "Then, after one hour maybe, we start again."

I argue that we will be hiking in the dark, but he assures me it will stay light until nine o'clock.

He stands and his body sways. He grips the table with his hands, and I reach over to steady him. He sits down.

"Is okay, Lindsey. Is the wine. Only this."

DUSK SETTLES in over the Ligurian cliffs. Roberto sleeps. We are not far from Vernazza. From where we are perched, I can now see the village jut out into the sea. The stone tower of Santa Margherita rising over the Piazza Guglielmo Marconi. A mosaic of rooftops covers its narrow streets.

I watch Roberto sleep and touch the camera again. But I don't dare raise it. His arms are so very thin. Instead, I take a different snapshot in my mind.

Vienna. We crossed the Ringstrasse. A light snow fell. We talked and laughed about our mutual dream to see Saint Petersburg in winter.

His face was white and gray, like the buildings and the snow. I wanted to rub the gray smudge on his forehead with the eraser tip of a pencil, make it all clean and healthy. I wanted to see the warm bronzed skin I saw in Greece only months earlier. I wanted to return to that moment when he held me close and I wondered if I should risk it.

At Café Sacher, a waiter wearing white gloves brought us coffee in thick ceramic cups. A small piece of chocolate on the saucer. Roberto gave me his because he knew how much I love chocolate.

We chatted with an American couple at the table alongside. They talked about the time they saw Leonard Bernstein conduct Mahler's *Fifth* at the Vienna Opera House. There'd been a small earthquake. Nothing serious, but the floors shook, and people ran for the exits. But the esteemed conductor stayed. He plunged into the music and directed his baton with an explosive rapture.

Afterwards he said, "I've always wanted to conduct Mahler and feel the earth move."

We laughed, imagining or wishing ourselves inside such a

story, but Roberto became serious and brought me back to the space the two of us filled.

"I have seen Bernstein leap into the air. I bought the most expensive ticket I could afford to get close at Lincoln Center so I could feel his volcanic spirit, his total abandonment to life and to the inevitability of death."

When he took leave from the table to smoke a cigarette outside, I felt dampness pool along my cheeks. Earlier he told me he'd decided to refuse treatments when we returned to New York the next day. I needed him to change his mind. I needed us to stay here in Vienna. No, I needed the days to stretch on so I could find the truth inside me about him.

The woman, Emma, said to me:

"You're in love with him, aren't you?"

"Yes." It was the first time I admitted it.

THE SUN DROPS into the sea as we descend into Vernazza. We cross a small bridge that arches over a stream. The clatter builds of voices, children racing home, plates and cutlery tossed on tables. I love the way the air smells of sweet florals preparing for sleep, of salt rising from the fishing boats below, of pungent cooking herbs. I see in Roberto's eyes something I've seen once. He smells, as I do, the savory focaccia Genovese he raved about that rainy day in London: the salty *fritelle al baccala* sizzling in olive oil stored in the cantina, the *trenette* dressed and twirled on a decades-old ceramic plate; the wooden table, scratched and scarred, beneath an open window, the complicit moon overhead; the sea below, dark and twisting. A frost suddenly brushes over me, and I hug my arms to my chest. I realize all at once: Roberto is returning *home.*

Roberto's father lives in a stone cottage near the quay. Roberto walks in first, pushing against the heavy wooden door. He drops into darkness. Only candles and a stone fireplace hold at bay a deathly blackness. A small, thin man sits in front of the flames, warming his hands. His fingers are long and transparent, like his son's. Roberto kneels beside him and places a hand on his shoulder.

The man doesn't turn, but his eyes start to crinkle and fill. If he had teeth, he would grind them.

Giving Roberto this moment, I walk out the back door. I sit on the steps in the garden and rest my head on my arms. My legs ache.

"Lindsey." I have no idea how much time has passed. Roberto sits beside me. I barely feel it. He's so light, there is no movement around him. Even the steady drone of crickets can't drown out the sound of his father crying inside the house.

"You are fine?" he asks me.

"Yes, I'm fine, but I'm tired."

"Me too."

"I was just thinking. Why don't we go to Portovenere by boat? I'd love to see these villages from a different place, from the sea looking up, instead of looking down from the hills."

He sighs, reaches for both my hands, and it is he who says:

"Lindsey, please listen."

I want to pull them away. I didn't want to listen. For once, just this once, I didn't want Roberto to be Roberto.

I try my best to look at him. I can't.

"I cannot finish."

Now I do look at him. Scared.

"I will stay in Vernazza," he says. "You can stay too until you need to leave for Milan. There is a train every morning at eight o'clock. I will take you to the station. But me, my journey finishes here."

"But we can continue! We can even take the train if it's easier."

He shakes his head. "You think that if I take the boat or train, it will not be so hard and I will not die so soon. Is true?"

"No. That's not it." Am I lying?

"It is. You want me to live longer than I can live."

"Of course I do! Why not? You have no idea how long it will be. We can finish the trip and we can go back to New York. If you have some treatments—"

Instead of answering, he pulls a flower from a low, hanging branch and strokes it under my nose.

I push his hand away.

"The least you can do is try to beat this." I reach for anger ferociously, like one does for a miracle, like I wish I'd reached for him. That's what hangs from a branch on a cliff. The miraculous in the face of the evident. I will grab it, retrieve it, not fall. Retrieve him.

"What about Portovenere? You've always wanted to go back there. Now's your chance."

I bribe and beg with every ounce of energy. The wind keeps swinging the branch out of reach. I grab, but my hand holds only air.

"So, if I cannot see it, then you must see it. For me, you must go to Portovenere."

"I'm not finishing this trip without you."

"No, maybe not now. But some time, you must do this journey, backwards, from Portovenere to Monterosso, on foot. You must finish, for me."

∼

WHAT IS it about gay men? My eyes are swollen, in rage and pain, while the next morning's train hurtles to Milan. Why do we love them, share our dreams with them? Only to be waved off at a station, where they turn away and move into another life. Why does the stupid sex thing always get in the way? Couldn't we just live together like a bored married couple? I had it all planned out. We could each have a lover on the side. But, in the evening, in our home by the fire in Vernazza or Vienna, with a beautiful aria playing, we would share dreams, like that dream of Saint Petersburg with the falling snow.

One can't dream like that with straight men.

TWO YEARS LATER, I no longer fight to forget the wish to dream with that ferocity. I stand at the edge of a stone promontory. The coast at Portovenere is grayer than I imagined it, but the adjoining seas, the Ligurian and the Mediterranean, undulate with glints of deep blue under a full moon. To the east, lights flicker from the port at La Spezia. More lights snap on as the Ligurians wake up one at a time. Somewhere by the shore, a fisherman is sorting his nets. I am the lone hiker waiting for the first light of dawn and, thus, to begin: new boots, a knapsack full of provisions, my notepad. Have I prepared myself well? I glance back down the dark vertiginous path. It starts at the city's center, marking the head of the trail as it winds its way around the hills of the Cinque Terre through all five villages to Monterosso to the north.

In my notepad is Roberto's map, drawn in his hand.

The sun is rising slowly. The sea air whips in around my face.

I glance out, not down. The panorama in front of me stops my breath. It's different. All feels different. The cold wind wraps me in its embrace.

I dig my heels into the earth, and I ground myself there. Siena, the crash of the Aegean against our bare legs, Viennese chocolate passed from his hand to mine, the sprinkles of early light along that sunny path re-traveled now in cold and mist, this time alone but not entirely. Do the ghosts of our soulmates travel with us? They do now as I sink in the damp earth, inhale the floral smokiness of tonka bean, the renegade chocolate once touching my lips. I feel every part of me pulse and expand outward. I'm aware of blood and muscle and skin, an engulfing erotic sensation, one I had craved but denied myself. It now enters every awakened pore of my being. I take in the panorama. It's winter so the sun is low, the skies a gray wash over blue, but the water in rapid flow; the paths are less a welcome than a call to action. The muted palette allows for open thought, for the pursuit of answers. I sit down on the rock, rest my head against the olive tree, and I know, without question and in this moment, that I am experiencing true joy.

THAT's the last I remember of Roberto, until now. Until I stand where he stood, facing a grim possibility, ravaged by regret. That one time. I had the chance to love him. I ran away, or he did. I realize the grief has consumed me these thirty years. Where did they go? Where did the rains of the tears fall? Where did the sprouts of rationalization lift out of the earth of regret? It's so easy to walk backwards into those past mistakes. Could I not walk it back further to a time when I could have saved him?

Perhaps we would have that other life, a paradigm that defies the norms of sanctioned sexuality. Did they even have a basis in fact? Why be male or female? Why name our gender? Why name our race? To what purpose? Why do the plagues swoop down and kill those who love with the same volcanic passion as Bernstein leaping into the air when he played Mahler and the earth moved?

As the world opens up, resistance disguised as caution pushes me back. The young men then. I, a straight woman, did not fear the virus that killed them. I cast myself into the hallowed halls of social rights advocate, consoled I did my part. I attended the memorials, threw rose petals, sent balloons into the air, painted rainbows on my window. But did I work from the center of the heart circle in Roberto's drawing, straight through the head's thinking, and into meaningful action? If I had stayed the course the way I unflinchingly did two years after his death, along the path he made me promise to take, where would I be today?

What could I have changed?

I think about the voices that pushed back against him. Love who and how you want to love, but be careful; keep the secret until you can tell it.

Why does their fear take precedence over a human right to love?

Even today I don't know.

I do know that I am, once again, in an enviable place.

I know my illness is not a stigma or a death warrant.

I know I have not been forced to risk as others have.

I know I've been given the gift of survival while others have not.

I know each successive pandemic will have a different cast of victims.

And for all those reasons I need the answer.

The path is clear.

I must shoot forward from the center of the heart circle with the singular, disruptive thrust of a spacecraft on its way to the moon. On the way, I will look out not down. Only at the stars.

IT WAS THE YEAR

It was the year of Yoji Yamamoto and Sonja Rykiel. That year, she stayed at the Hôtel Saint James et Albany, where her room overlooked a courtyard café and breakfast came to her every morning in a *panier* filled with warm croissants, buttered baguette, raspberry preserves. Covering the lushness was a blue-checkered cloth.

It was the year her hairdresser met her in Paris, where they drank Cristal at La Coupole while cutting her hair pixie short. Not Imane short, but she had neither the same perfect bone structure nor that forcible will.

Paris and Tokyo toggled in her esprit like her left and right arms picking up the asymmetrical linen shirts of Issey Miyake and the tailored shifts at YSL. The world was still enthralled by the Japanese economic miracle, by the power of consensus and collaborative endeavor, by startling innovation and bold technologies. It spawned workshops and focus groups, probing the secrets of this quiet Asian island and its meteoric rise into the pinnacles of business management theory studied at Harvard and Wharton and promising productivity. It spawned creativity in design and a fascination for meditative living.

It was the year a definitive Japanese style ethos, nourished by the ancient practices of *ikigai* and *shinrin-yoku,* emerged on the world stage wrapped in frenetic and timeless fervor.

She dressed without fear of corporate retribution in all black with a green line painted under her eyebrow—she followed the Kabuki-style makeup of Serge Lutens. She drank Cristal with him, too, at Le Grand Vefour, his favorite restaurant. He flew in from the Orient, when we would say *Orient,* his Palais-Royal boutique as yet an intent, and he smelled of the night, doused in his Nombre Noir from a flask of black hexagon. A calibrated sensuality one parceled out at one's pleasure.

It was all about will and what one did with it, said Imane.

"*Vous avez changez de tête,*" she said when she saw Arianna's new short do, and she accompanied Arianna to Christian Dior on Avenue Montaigne to buy the fur-trimmed velvet wedding dress. A winter wedding in New York called for belle-epoque adornment.

It was the year they ate *poulet frites* at the Café des Beaux Arts because the art students went there. One could eat for cheap, the wine always good. It was the year they lied to their boyfriends. Instead of going to a movie, they went to the hammam in the *cinque,* where they walked around naked and lavished layers of oils onto glistening skin. One night, along the-then bohemian Rue du Bac, they found a tiny traditional French restaurant that was "homo," as Imane liked to say, as it didn't attract many straight people. She was quite content to make love with men or women, especially on a Sunday when most of them went to church.

It was the year of Tunisian barbecue and chocolate sausages made with pig's blood in the back alleys of Montmartre. It was the year of Left Bank lingering to summon up de Beauvoir and Sartre and Baldwin and Hemingway. It was the year newly minted Parisian friends from North Africa described the cuisine of the *pieds noirs*, of *couscous roulé* a certain way, spices she never understood. It was the year of kir royale with an Egyptian diplomat, down the stairs from Boulevard Saint-Germain at a restaurant called Le Petite Cour.

It was the year when the Hôtel Bristol welcomed her arrivals with Louis XVI sleeping rooms and silver trays. Under a chandelier, she dined with Françoise Hardy; she breakfasted with the legend Helmut Schmidt. It was the year of foreign dreamscapes mixed in with unflagging work. Of questions postponed, temptations rebuffed.

It was the year of long walks along the Faubourg Saint-Honoré when the dollar was king and shopping did not cost her year's salary. Linen dresses, belts and sandals, the sleek Angelo Tarlazzi evening dress with a huge taffeta bow. A Cerruti suit, pillowy blouses, ostrich flats from a shop by La Madeleine.

An assignation for chocolates at the gilded Fauchon.

She first met Imane and her female companion Paule over jazz at the Caveau de la Huchette. Of strong bone structure and doleful eyes, Imane originated from Algeria, her father killed in the Algerian war. Of her mother, she said nothing. Her brother drove very fast but always managed to skid to a stop before running someone over. And he brought tiny bottles of champagne to welcome Arianna back to Paris month after month, year after year, and introduced her to his friend Hassan, who told her she reminded him of an Indian actress. That she was more "Orientale" than "Occidentale," and she liked it. She found him too earnest.

It was the year she crossed the Pacific on Singapore Airlines into Tokyo, of bright lights along Shinjuku and dark hotels with sunken bathtubs, where silence and minimalism quieted her anxiety and gave vent to plans and programs, the imagination of cool logic. It was the era of shopping Rei Kawakubo and Kenzo in the Ginza, where stores morphed into the fantastical: geometric spaces, cutouts along the floor, smooth white marble, gray leather, softness. It was the year of the Japanese Women's Marathon and the butterflies of Hanae Mori. It was the year the fashion world gave birth to courage, unleashed by permeable borders.

She sent Imane photos, and they talked on the phone, she with her sake, Imane with champagne, drunk always from a flute. Her cheekbones luminous under candlelight.

It was the year she imagined what would happen to her Algerian friend in her tiny flat in Montparnasse.

It was the year of pleated and deconstructed garments, about the ease of fabric without restrictions, of perpetual, mystical movement, of sensations without a name. A blind tasting of essences as if one were always in flight, circling the island upon which one was about to land. And the passport meant nothing. It was simply a photo of the traveler who would one day leave, changed forever, and reach in the darkness to grab at the one defining characteristic of who she'd become.

It was the year it snowed in Nikko. She found a small teahouse serving dark, creamy chocolate, and as she held the cup between her palms, felt her heart flutter for reasons unknown. Her friend had blonde hair, and all the children in the small town wanted their photos taken with her. They shared cameras with frosty mittens and bowed as they'd learned to do in sleek corporate offices overlooking the Ginza.

Nothing would be the same.

It was the year Roman Polanski starred in *Amadeus* in the Théâtre Marigny, and she walked back to the Bristol in the rain along the deserted Champs Élysées and the Rue du Faubourg Saint-Honoré, lingering in front of Hermès and wondering what pieces of herself would be left behind should she ever depart.

It was the year Paris was at her doorstep and Tokyo the next port of entry and New York a spot of repose from which to gather up images and textures, as if they were all simply fabrics waiting to be touched and worn. Ceramic and lacquer, the fluid modernity of Miyake; bodies as sculpture, shapes in nylon and bone. Luminous fragrances wafting from flacons of etched glass. We felt inside nature, interpreted by these masters of organic design in cosmopolitan centers tethered to their natural world.

It was the year we celebrated the New Year on a New York rooftop singing Edith Piaf's *"Non, je ne regrette rien."* Fireworks burst into prisms of promise over Central Park.

It was the year Arianna flew into Paris once again, another in a string of countless times, but now, Imane had disappeared. It was the year the Towers fell as she walked from the Left Bank to the Right, the tragedy unfurling an ocean away as she slid under the stained-glass dome of Galeries Lafayette. The sky was impossibly blue, behind her the black tower of Montparnasse, the Seine, the Eiffel Tower, the expanse of parks and boulevards as she crossed the bridges, unaware of the new world order meeting her next time at the conference table. Bliss, then crash. Parisians repeatedly pushing redial buttons on their cellphones that night at Buddah Bar, wine glasses untouched. Who was safe? Who had been inside when the planes struck? Who was yet to return home? How many of her friends had taken off their high heels to walk across the Williamsburg Bridge, and how dark were the streets.

Their waiter at Deux Magots remembered. He brought her the Courvoisier she and Imane always ordered as they smoked Galois on the terrace in matching leather jackets. Always that better future beckoned, the one that was yet to come. He rubbed her shoulder and said no charge as her tears fell and wouldn't stop.

It was the year Arianna married, wearing the dress Imane had convinced her to buy. She returned home and moved into a condominium with her husband. Since that year, she and Imane have never seen one other again.

THE FIFTH SISTER

"She'll never go for it," says Victoria, eyes traversing two screens. Travel itinerary in Word. Budget on Excel.

"I'll convince her," replies Angela, *la giornalista*. The only one their mother listens to.

She's the first to grab the moka pot making its familiar rumble on the stove. The three sisters, including Eva, Lila's youngest, take the same space in turn or, maybe more exactly, each as if it is her own. Angela covers her face with her hands, overwhelmed momentarily by what they aim to convince Lila of, before starting to pour the coffee. Eva lifts the curtain onto the garden of the Astoria apartment. Tomato plants in full view. Sighs and silence compete with the hum of their mother's sewing machine in the next room.

Without needing to ask, Angela pours out for everyone their third espresso of the morning. Into tiny Ginori cups the viscous liquid pours, that old china still intact. Not a single chip all these years. A gift from Nonna Laura for Angela's first wedding. There is something luxurious about lifting one of these yellow and white striped cups from its sculpted saucer, also yellow and white but in a floral pattern. Each sip feels like a mini celebration. Bequeathed by a *contadina*, a woman who worked the fields, who never left her village, but whose presence of mind saw the light in every object. The sisters felt its rays across oceans each time they opened a package from her.

"When forces intersect, she will." Eva turns from the window back to the garden blooming on the table. She rests a barely flowering lily stem upside down against the edge of a low ceramic bowl and measures hikai, the third part of her ikebana arrangement. The tip of its stem is cut on a diagonal so as to touch the inside of the vase and rest at a fifteen-degree angle tilting forward. With not so much as a frown, Eva coaxes the white petals to open and look her in the eye. She ignores her sisters and adjusts two thin branches so that they scrawl like lightning bolts over the flowering hikai. There is open space between them. Its symbolism, according to ikebana practices, means the future is open to possibility. She tilts her hikai upward.

Though the precision of symbolism that ikebana affords has made Eva a fast devotee of the art, she remains at heart a person who prefers to stare out, which she now does again. She takes a moment to stare past the shoots pushing up in the window box to a time they didn't argue as much, to the corner across the street where her family's bakery once stood. It's a pharmacy now, but memories hold fast; the scent of anise, of Mama kneading dough and handing her fluffy pinches of it, her father selecting the correct cookie assortment from the glass display case to place inside the white cardboard box Angela lined with tissue paper.

She rests her elbows on the windowsill. This brings her an inch closer to her wish, that they could all be in the back office of the bakery again, dipping Sicilian *cuccidati* into their caffè latte, fingers all gooey with crumbs and rainbow sprinkles.

In the meantime, Victoria keeps staring at the numbers. She alone manages and massages the miscellaneous account that will cover this trip, including business class tickets for them all—for the daughters to stand, to pull compression socks over their mother's legs; for the children to prop up pillows and avert clots. Only it will be Victoria who does all this, so she chooses two seats where they can lie next to each other and hold hands.

One day in the not-too-far future, this will be the privilege she misses the most.

Angela, with insouciance, will instead sneak into the first-class bar to drink cocktails and flirt with a sartorially correct stranger. She'll search for her signature perfume from the duty-free catalogue and exit the plane with a flacon of Bulgari Black and the well-dressed guy's phone number.

Eva will choose to sit the furthest away. The minute they reach cruising altitude and the seatbelt signs go off, she'll pull open the flatbed, drop down, cover herself with the blanket she knitted herself, and sleep through the night. She will wake up fresh and enlightened as if emerging from an Indian ashram.

And she, Victoria? When they disembark, she will summon the wheelchair. She will push while her distracted sisters drag their four carry-ons along the tentacled retail therapy corridors of Fiumicino. Angela will have them stop every few steps and, to their mother's delight, point out a handbag, a Missoni scarf, the shape of the newest heel on a pair of gleaming leather boots. She and Mama will want to look, touch, try on, but Victoria will order them to move quickly as she navigates around the crowd. She'll make sure they all have their documents and take money out of the *bancomat* to save on change fees in banks. She'll ask if they want a *cornetto* or a *panino* or need to stop in the restroom. Eva will make them wait as she grabs her first espresso at the bar and flirts with the male barista, even though she's gay. She gets her kicks doing that.

Victoria will keep the operation humming as she always does. She doesn't mind, she says. She knew caregiving would extract from her body and her spirits. She hadn't banked on losing her identity. She envied the freedom of friends and of strangers posting Instagram photos of sunsets and of ocean waves rolling over pink sands. They traveled on a whim, met friends for coffee, discussed Vermeer and Calder at the Frick. Their streamlined bathrooms didn't have a raised toilet seat and grab bars along the walls. Their entryways didn't resemble the waiting room of an orthopedic hospital.

And they hadn't moved back to their childhood home in Astoria. To Victoria she has gone full circle, back to where she started, as if all she'd accomplished had been an illusion.

"It'll take a lot to convince her." Angela shrugs when Eva suggests this. "Maybe tell her it's the last time she may ever see her sisters."

"Thank you for the dark point of view." Victoria sweeps plant stems and leaves off the table and into a paper bag. Eva is never neat when she's creating.

"It's not a revelation to her. She's ninety-seven."

"And still working."

"Is that a good thing?'

"It's what she wants."

"Until she falls and is confined to a wheelchair. Then what will you do?"

"What I've been doing for the past ten years."

Every morning Victoria, now a widow, as well as a retired ER nurse, fastens the clasp of her mother's pearls around the neck of her black coat-check attendant uniform and walks her to the bus stop, where Lila takes the first seat and swirls around just long enough for her daughter to wave her good-bye. Then, in the evening, she picks Mama up in a taxi. The fare is almost a day's wages. But work is Mama's lifeblood. *Consider it my theater ticket,* she says as she counts the singles she's made in tips and secures them in her pocket with a safety pin.

Angela eyes the moka once more in her sister's hand. "You're lucky," she says softly. "She's with you every day. When you walk through that door, she looks at you with so much love every time. I'm jealous of that, actually."

"I know, but one day..." Victoria fills her sister's cup.

In her mind she revisits the ritual. She enters, closes the door, takes off her shoes. She drops her keys into the small clay plate she made in grade school. It sits on top of a lace doily. She places her handbag, her phone, and her sunglasses alongside. She kisses her mother on the forehead and takes her hands in her own. "She wants to live her life fully until the end. I have to respect that."

"Well, I'm glad we're going, whether it's the right time or not." Eva has returned to the table with a sprig of basil in her soil-splattered hand. It's deliciously fragrant as only fresh-cut basil can be. She hands it to both her sisters.

And there is no further discussion.

This time, because the three sisters know it will be the last time, this trip ups the ante of importance. So, on the evening of their departure, while her sisters waited at the door, Victoria zips up her suitcase and slides the four passport cases into her carry-on. Lila watches to ensure Victoria places her phone, computer, chargers, and important items neatly in their proper place, that Victoria locks up where she has to. The lines around

Lila's eyes soften at the unexpected comfort of relinquishing control.

When Victoria is ready, Lila shouts, "*Forza,*" at her younger daughters and tilts her head to the bags.

ON THEIR FIRST joyous morning in Rome, they are giddy, ravenous with happiness. Laughter flows so naturally here. Maybe it was the irony and cadence in the taxi driver's voice, the swirl of traffic around Piazza Venezia, or simply the ever-spry Roman light.

They don't argue about the best place for caffè and *cornetti.* It has to be Sant'Eustachio because Angela confirmed it still serves its renowned caffe in the butter yellow cups Lila loves. The waiter brings plump *cornetti alla crema* for Angela and Lila and *integrali* filled with honey for Eva and Victoria.

"Are you still sorry we got you here?" asks Angela.

"Yes. But none of you will listen." Lila scoops some cream from her plate.

"You know, Mama, I only recently realized you had a sweet tooth."

"We never had sweets in the house growing up," chimes in Victoria.

"Yeah, our friends couldn't figure out why we went to Mary's for Oreos when our parents owned a bakery."

"I wanted you to learn to eat right so you would have a long healthy life like mine. My job is done now, so now I will eat what I want."

"Expedient, I'd say."

"*Per forza!* This crema is divine!"

As if he anticipated a renewed order, their waiter brings a second *cornetto alla crema* to the oldest woman at the table.

"*Lo offro io,*" he says, hand on his chest. I offer it to you—the Italian equivalent of *it's on me.*

The sisters are ready for the inevitable. Lila will engage with Paolo as he recounts how he has moved here from Ragusa, where his parents own a pastry shop that makes the best pistachio cream for their *tartufo* and, not surprisingly, *cuccidati.*

"In my bakery in Astoria," she tells him, "my husband put a map of Italy on the office wall, and next to the regions and cities, he drew pictures of cookies: *struffoli* from Napoli, *le nevole* from our Abruzzo, *osssi dei morti* from Piemonte, *zaletti* from Venezia—these were Vittoria's favorite—and *occhi di bue* from Trentino-Alto Adige."

"*Davvero?* Tell me more. How do you find the iron to make the design for *le nevole*? It is impossible to find. When you order it, it takes months to arrive."

"It was hard even then." Lila's head snaps with its nod. "And many young Abruzzians never heard of them. I don't blame them because they are a bit boring. After the war, it was the only dessert you could make with just a few ingredients. I still prefer the *ossi dei morti* biscotti. In Sicilia you make them even better. You coat them with chocolate. You understand sweets. My girls got lots of cavities from your *cuccidati.*"

There is nowhere to hurry now. Time takes its time, like that moment on a camera lens. Learn your subject first. Then capture it. Eva's the one living the metaphor. She raises her camera and clicks into permanence first her mother's face and then her hand tearing away at the cornetto. The veins on those hands raise up from the flesh. The daughters don't remember a time when the veins weren't there. Surely at one point their mother had smooth, youthful hands. She'd always taken care of them. But she never stopped using them. Victoria sees the same bluish swirls under her own skin.

"So! Where to today?" asks Eva as Paolo clears their plates and hands a small yellow flower, a mimosa, to Lila.

"Mama wants to shop. Where to, Mama?"

"Piazza di Spagna *per forza*. And Gianicolo. We must walk up to Gianicolo."

They have this one full day together before they leave for Abruzzo early the next morning. There they will be surrounded by aunts and cousins and old friends. But for now, the hours of just they four are precious.

"Okay, ladies, time to split up!" Angela takes her mother's arm and waves Victoria away. "I'll take over from here. You two run along. Meet at Gianicolo at one o'clock."

"You need that much time?" Eva asks.

"We're going to Via Condotti! We'll need an hour in just one shoe store!"

Indeed, her mother had abruptly stepped into the street, forcing a *motorino* to swerve and zoom past. Two of the sisters gasped. Not Eva, who pointed to Lila's razor-sharp focus on a pair of classic riding boots in the window of a small and barely noticeable boutique.

"No stopping her now," says Victoria. "And we're not even in Piazza di Spagna yet. You two fashionistas had getter get a move on."

"You too! *Vai*, Victoria!" Her mother waves her away. "Go to Via Margutta. If you see a pair of earrings, I will buy them for you. And you need some pearls." She frowns at her daughter's naked lips. "Buy some lipstick, too! You're beginning to look like a nun!"

Victoria feels the heat rise in her cheeks. But Lila isn't finished.

"Remember the *sarta* at the corner of Via Margutta near Hotel Manfredi. Marcella is her name. She can make you something nice. You wear the same things all the time. Too much black. And she can pick out shoes for the outfit, too, and a nice scarf."

"Ooh. I remember," says Angela. "She was amazing. You came in with a fabric, and she designed the dress and chose everything that went with it—the shoes, the accessories. The whole look. I hope she's still there."

"She most probably is," sighed Victoria. "Can I go now?"

"Go! And do what I said!"

"Okay, Mama. I got it! Goodbye."

She struts away and this time she does not look back. She walks fast, in a fury until she arrives, earlier than planned, along the quiet pedestrian streets. Here she slows her pace. She is free. All that opens up in front of her affirms it. So much so, she takes in every languid curve of road, every coral and rose variation in the colored stone, a trellis of vines swaying over a travertine street sign, the sensation of raised cobblestones under her feet, and voices of people greeting, conversing, saying goodbye, all in her native language. The first language she'd ever learned. She stares for a long time at a gleaming violin in a gallery window.

So, she buys some freshwater pearl drop earrings and, suppressing a giggle, lifts open a vintage silver compact to apply the bold velvet red lipstick, filling in the bow of her lips now outlined in a dark pencil. She purses and blots with a tissue. She barely remembers when she last did this with such attention. And it is worth it. She tightens the belt of her white jacket and almost dances down the street toward Marcella's elusive studio with the swagger of years past.

Meanwhile, enjoying her own freedom from the opinions

of her sisters, Angela slowly escorts Lila past each elegant Via Condotti storefront. Along the way, markers of Angela's past. Her first patent leather T-strap flats when she was twelve, her four-inch-high scarlet pumps at thirteen, a shantung silk suit many years later and still in her closet, embroidered by Mama to cover moth holes. She never threw anything away. Mending a garment made it more beautiful. Eva compared it to Japanese kintsugi, the art of repairing broken pottery pieces with gold paint. She wishes she'd brought the suit jacket with her, to wear again, in this place.

On the morning they bought the suit, her father took them to Caffè Greco, where he and Lila had befriended the manager. As merchants themselves, they understood the art of hospitality and the work and sacrifice it required. Something else, too. They missed the bakery. On the day they locked it up, rolled down the gates for the last time, and handed over the keys, they couldn't speak. It was the first time they both skipped dinner. Victoria had reheated the leftovers, Angela set the table, Eva lit a candle, and the girls dined in silence. It was the beginning of a long, dark period in their lives.

Mama tightens her grip around her middle daughter's arm at the sight of pink azaleas scrolling down the *scalinata* of Piazza di Spagna, The memory explodes. That first time she and Massimo raced up the steps, each trying to beat the other to the top, where they kissed over and over again. When they thought their hearts would burst. Then, their last trip to Rome together, this time with their grown-up daughters, both she and Massimo in their seventies. Angela took their photo as they stepped arm in arm down the *scalinata*.

Angela remembers taking the photograph, too. How it must have touched them, she believes, to re-enter Rome decades later and relive their youth here, as flawed as it had been!

"Youth is a beautiful time," her father once said. "Even when it's not perfect, it promises perhaps someday it will be."

Her mother, however, is now staring single-mindedly into windows of the Genny boutique.

"This is where you bought that shantung suit with the leopard-print voile blouse. Very chic, very sexy."

"You convinced me to buy it. Every time I wear it, I think of Rome. You know what I've always wanted to do?"

"There are many things you want to do. What are you waiting for?"

"I want to take you to Paris with me, only for two days. That's all."

Lila gives her the look.

Ensuing silence speaks of the loss ahead.

A red-haired girl kicks a soccer ball and runs after it. Lila claps. "Brava!" The girl hugs the ball to her chest and nods her thanks before skipping away.

The magnificent *scalinata* draws closer. Angela's thirteen again. Or she's twenty-one, or twenty-five. Those times. She wants to relive them the way her parents did the last time they were all here together.

"Wear the suit."

"I will."

"With the sexy blouse. Nothing boring."

"Got it."

"Wear it in Paris and go to the Bon Marché. Buy yourself something nice there, from me."

Angela needs a distraction so her mother can't see her eyes.

"Buy something new there as a gift from me. Like old

times, only in a different city. In Paris, *your* favorite place. Rome is mine."

"It's a promise."

"But go alone. Travel alone. You can do it. *Coraggio!* If you go with a man, which I don't recommend, go with someone decent."

Longing and mischief in her voice. How they battle inside her. Young Lila advising the old. They are one and the same now.

"I hear you. But now *you* need to shop."

"Why do you think I came?"

So now Angela has her own conversation with the street.

Via Condotti, how often have you answered questions for us? You were the center of each family visit to this city. We walked four and five across along your elegant streets, talking along the way. You are aptly named—Condotti—the conduits drawing water from the city to the baths of Agrippa. You were for our family the conduit of our thoughts and dreams, expressions of all we wanted to experience and achieve, when the world felt so open and vibrant, when everything seemed possible. So here we are again staring up at the fragrant scalinata, *only two of us now.*

Providence steps in. As it always does, here in this spot. They turn the corner, and in front of them is Mama's favorite leather store.

LILA

WE'RE in the leather shop across from the Fontana della Barcaccia. I see a leather shoulder bag in a biscuit color with braided, caramel-colored handles. I like its rectangular shape.

It's modern and different. It's called Vittoria. It's like her. Understated and practical, more beautiful than it realizes.

I don't care who watches me. I see Angela become distracted as I lift the bag from the glass shelf, rest my cane on a chair. I hold it with both hands by my side, then on the crook of my arm. I move it to my shoulder, checking how it looks in the mirror. I keep my balance as I ruffle through the compartments inside. This is important for Victoria. She carries so much with her.

The mirror reminds me I'm old, but this bag makes me feel young again. That wonder. That passion we were never afraid to pursue. Before regrets. Before desires became memories.

And now, as Angela is distracted by wallets and cellphone cases, I remember that time. If only to hold onto it for a few minutes. When I was young, and years before I married Massimo, I would take off my sandals and dip my feet into the cold waters of the fountain just outside. It's made of travertine, so my hand always slid along its edges. It chilled the devil on hot days when the temperatures reached forty degrees. The *carabinieri* would wink at my defiance and light their cigarettes as they passed. I flirted back. One *carabiniere* with such clear green eyes gave me a flower.

My father warned me not to talk to strangers in Rome. It was a city of danger and temptation. Thieves and kidnappers lurked within her side streets and inside the stores I shopped along Via del Corso. He ranted fables of rape and necks snapped. He wanted to snuff the fire in my eyes to flee. The burning fire to live out my adolescent fervor without limits. I would escape the predictability and the monotony of our village. The life of a *contadina,* the life of my mother Laura, was of no interest to me. Aside from our alleys of vines, there was no place for me to run free. No place there I would miss.

This leather shop felt like my own private palazzo when I walked in, the wildflower still in my hair.

I have a confession. Even the girls don't know. I slept with that *carabiniere*. It was liberation for me. And it was worth the aftermath, the slap across my face by Massimo on my wedding night. I knew I would always keep with me what he tried to destroy.

"Mama, look at this handbag." Angela holds up a small, black crossbody bag with a gold-link chain. That girl has always had an eye for style. Many years ago, I bought her a small purse made entirely of tortoise shell. In my day we called it *osso*.

I would prefer to stay here instead of going back to Avezzano and Antrosano. The small house where Massimo and I started our married life will have been sold. I hear from my sister that a pizzeria has replaced it. Would it had burned to the ground. I have no fond memories of it. Domenica's, where the line for the only phone in town formed every Sunday morning, is now, imagine, a TIM cell phone store. Clothes still dry on lines across balconies because we Italians know dryers ruin them. My daughters should do the same. Yes, they live in apartments, but what does it take to buy one of those foldable racks and open a window? In Antrosano, people still beat rugs from on high. That balcony. Vittoria threw her lunchbox over it, declaring she didn't want *frittata*, she wanted *mortadella*. I don't blame her now. What was I thinking? Probably about more dangerous things. About what there was in the house to eat. Massimo would take the food to his mother. So, we had nothing, Vittoria and me. But my mother would bring us fresh eggs and vegetables and a plucked chicken to make broth. To make me strong for when he came home. He's gone from my life ten years now. I cried when he died. I pound my fists against the marble engraved with his name in the mausoleum. But I don't miss him. I admit it now.

He changed, was filled with regret in the end. I lost so many years, though.

Eva

THE *PIZZAIOULO* IS FROM TUNIS. He wears a yellow and black braided bracelet around his thin wrist, and it's what I look at as he pounds and lifts the pizza, proving one doesn't have to be born Italian to get it right. The Pinsa Romana is different from other pizzas, he tells me. One uses more water. He lets me pinch a piece of the dough. Go ahead and taste, he says. And I do, and it's soft and lightly salted, like the dough my mother makes but so much fluffier. He's staring at me through violet-gray eyes. A color I've not seen before.

I show him how my bracelet matches his. I was there, too. In Tunis. Other worlds for me, not only Italy. Places where I feel more alive.

I want some wine but perhaps it is too early. And I wonder if it's to forget how time passes, how life will be when she leaves it. I don't see a space in that future, or newly found freedom. I see a giant fortress that traps me inside.

For once I will not want to run and jump as she always encouraged me to do. She was the first to know I was different. She knew Papa's flirtation was a way to shame me into becoming normal like Angela, everyone's favorite, but I saw how he looked at Angela and it made me want to throw up.

Victoria

They were the five *-inas*. Rosalina, Adelina, Angelina, Delfina, and Lila—the fifth *-ina*, who wasn't. She was simply Lila the sister who left for a new life on a separate continent. The one whose scandalous secrets shadowed Nonna Laura's huge but never drafty stone house. In the highest heels she could find, that fifth Lila walked the dusty road past the cackling chickens. She never wobbled. To see her now in thick sneakers and support hose is to wonder about her, before she married Massimo. He had dreams, and his prevailed. If I'd been her best friend, not her daughter, I would have told her not to marry him.

I could have told her to leave him. But I was too young to know. At the ironing board in the dining room, she'd spray water, press the iron, fold our sheets and shirts so they would lie flat and even, pretty to hold. All the while she made points and warned me about consequences. I knew she knew what I did and shouldn't have done, what I was thinking, plotting, and planning to lie about. She'd been around betrayal her entire life. She knew where it hid. She knew when it was necessary.

I take her arm now for the long slow walk back down Via Condotti into Caffè Greco where she can relive more memories and Angela can set off to revisit some of her own.

Angela

Ah, the Pantheon. I need its geometric forms to center me here. When I was a child, I sat at that café table there with a sketchpad, a ruler, and a compass, and I tried to draw its triangles and circles and squares. I admired its strong unarticulated columns and battle-scarred pediment because, when you stepped back far enough, you saw the dome rise over it. The Pantheon is always true to itself.

That *cornetto alla crema* on Mama's plate. Her vitality as she scooped it up. A gelato for me now, why not? I choose pistachio and *nocciola*. Victoria and I once breakfasted on pizza followed by gelato. Such freedom. We never imagined then that time would pass this quickly. But I don't feel old here. Something stirs, and it's not only the jolt of espresso or the admiring male glances who remind me that I am not invisible. It's a sense of place. It says I belong here. This is why I move about so fluidly, why everything feels right.

Mama would order her gelato with *panna* and scoop it up with a small spoon as if every small mouthful were as precious as caviar eggs. She knows how to stop for life's important moments. She also knows to spring forth from a momentary respite with urgency and purpose, beauty in her purview.

Victoria lets her cut up vegetables for minestrone with a table knife because now that she is on blood thinners, she can't handle anything sharp. She still makes each piece of carrot, celery, zucchini symmetrical. Mama folds their laundry in such a pretty way as if T-shirts and socks were cashmere sweaters at Bergdorf's. Her perfectly manicured hands. They make art of everything she touches.

Victoria has had so many moments with Mama. But now as I stare at the fabrics and a tape measure inside the windows of a *sartoria*, I think of her as if she were young again. I'm drawn to a young girl stepping up onto a stool as the *sarta* measures the hem of artfully torn vintage jeans. The girl chatters happily with the seamstress. As I watch, the memory of the dress Mama made me sprints forward. I wore it for the SnowBall at the Sherry-Netherland, when I was the age this girl is now. We, Mama and I, shopped together for the silver-embroidered white brocade. Oh, the fabrics department then! Rows and rows of textures, colors, rickrack trim. Shimmering satins, multiple cottons; poplin, Batiste handkerchief linen, dotted Swiss. The woolens in bouclé, gabardine, crepe, and ottoman. Mom knew all the names. The brocade felt smooth and strong as she held it up to my neck to test its reflections. I never stood still enough, so she would glare me into conformity. She always stood straight as a sunflower stalk in mid-afternoon. It's only now that her back curves, and I know it humiliates her, but we humans, even as we fight back, sometimes need to give a little.

But I was telling you about the dress! The finished dress and its swing coat fell long and graceful. Eyes trailed me as I walked into the fake pine and tinsel-glittered room, erasing my adolescent insecurities, annoying little cartoon characters I finally had the presence to shoo away. It was the era of Loretta Young sweeping into a room in a gorgeous dress, her eyes ablaze. Mama made me a queen that day. She'd helped me realize being different was cooler than being like everyone else. It's still my mantra.

I've finished my gelato, I will now go to Termini to pick up our train tickets for tomorrow. For the first time, I will not be guiding Mama in-between pedestrians along a busy Via Nazionale, past multiple shops and *saldi* signs, past our favorite trattoria down the stairs from the street where they made, according to her, the tagliatelle with veal ragù that could, on a minor level, rival her own. I will walk quickly around the *fontana* and not glance at the bench where she would sit for five minutes to rest her feet and look out in awe of her beloved Rome. She had such light in her eyes, strangers would stop to speak to her, and as she spoke, they too marveled at what they had never truly seen.

No, I will keep going and then make my way across the Ponte Sant'Angelo and towards Gianicolo.

VICTORIA

SO HERE WE all are at Gianicolo, the quiet eighth hill of Rome. We walk up the steep, meandering paths from the west of the river to the *colle,* from which all of Rome opens its arms. *Welcome home.*

Mama leans heavily on her cane as she pushes up the incline, and I wish we'd taken the bus to the center of Garibaldi Square, as Eva so wisely suggested. But she insists on walking, so we proceed slowly, arm in arm, Eva and Angela forging ahead. As usual I toggle behind with Mama on my arm, and along the way I remember we are steps from Trastevere and my student apartment there, when she flew over to meet me every summer because Rome was the only city she'd wanted to live in her entire life.

Gianicolo, how that name reverberates with my mother's memories of unmitigated freedom. On Gianicolo, she could be Lila. She didn't hide her cigarettes, her silk lingerie, and her copies of Anaïs Nin. It was the place in which she could breathe in the air of desire. The place where she escaped for a brief time, only to be forced to come home.

"I ran away with two dresses, two skirts, one lace blouse, folded the right way in that beat-up leather suitcase."

"You still have that suitcase."

It doesn't have wheels. It's heavy even when empty, but she carried it back and forth to Italy for years.

"I had a job there at the Ospedale del Bambino Gesù, to help take care of a girl with polio."

"I know, Mama, I know." She tells the same story. The regret feels raw and fresh each time. My sisters are far ahead of us.

"I was going to be a nurse, Victoria, like you. I was so good as an apprentice, they wanted me to stay."

I squeeze her hand hard as if to press away all the shards of loss.

"Now I can't even walk up the hill. I can barely stand up. They were going to give me a modest salary and room and board inside a villa."

"Your father was worried about your safety."

"I was always safe. I know how to take care of myself. And she would watch over me!" She pointed to the statue of Anita Garibaldi on horseback.

"*Era una strega.*" To her a *strega*, a witch, is not the menace of misogynistic folklore but a shrewd, fearless woman.

"*Guarda!* She charges on that horse, pistol raised high, her baby on her arm. When I saw her then for the first time, I knew what I needed to do."

"You always know what you need to do, Mama."

I want my sisters to turn around and be a part of this conversation. "Hey! Are you two on your own private holiday?"

Angela rolls her eyes. Eva snaps a tree branch with her fingers.

"We want to take in the view."

"We didn't want to interrupt you."

"Well, you did. By walking away."

It was on this quiet hill and by this statue that young Lila formed her words and her thoughts, the shadows and shapes of them, the spine of her life's work. She knew then even before her father mandated her return, that she would build her own future amidst insults and setbacks. She would live in a large and glorious city with a history, be given a chance to see things anew.

You see, I believed my father loved her. How could I not? When he spoke about my mother, there was a luster in his eyes and words. He knew she was the unifying thread stitching, by hand, the possibilities and realized dreams for all of us. Only now do I see how strategic she was, putting together the broken pieces of shattered trust. I almost see them on the floor. Infidelity, disparagement, betrayal. I feel this more than my sisters do. They were born later. They didn't see what I saw.

My sisters leave us here on the hill. They run back down and split apart once again. Eva in the direction of Piazza di Spagna and Angela toward the Pantheon. I could resent them for leaving me here, her arm holding me in place. But I want this now. I don't pull away as I have in the past. This moment is worth the lost freedom, the narrowing of my world.

She taught me that the way out of malaise or inaction was to venture out beyond oneself. So now, I see what she sees. I see the expanse beyond Gianicolo, of Rome, of antiquity, of the Renaissance and the Baroque folding into modernity, centuries of building and rebuilding. In a flash, I get it. All of it. Amidst the stone and the green and the gasps of blue sky, I link arms with those who walked these trails centuries before me.

Lila continues to look up at the face of Anita Garibaldi and punches a fist in the air.

"This *strega* had to win. She was always about *la vittoria!* That's why I named you this!"

A group of tourists descends the hill, away from us and toward Trastevere. And we are once more—the two of us—alone together.

EVA

SAVE ME FROM THESE TWO. Victoria and Angela. Prima donnas. Each burnishing her victim credentials. I have to admit, they do a lot. Here I'm at Caffè Canova, enjoying the statues of the naked men. I laugh at how they preen. My *spremuta* is just right, naturally sweet and light, squeezed oranges from Sicilia perhaps, a place my father visited often, without us. I don't put sugar in my caffè, not since that day he rubbed my knee as we both sat at the bar in Avezzano, my hand holding the long spoon in midair. His touch made me nauseous. I put the spoon down. I drank it black. He mocked me, laughed. The laugh of victory. And that was always the point.

My sisters don't know this, and I will never tell. There is the tattoo of a flower on my arm. It's of a gardenia. My mother wore gardenia perfume whenever she and my father went out. It smelled awful. It smelled of his hands when he snuck into my room at night. I got the tattoo to remind me never to let a man touch me again.

ANGELA

MY SISTERS WILL NOT ASK why I retraced my steps to the Pantheon a second time, our train tickets in my purse. It was all so efficient at the station without Mom in tow. Uneventful, as well. How do I explain feeling disconnected? In line at the ticket counter, eyes fixed on my phone, scrolling in a zombie-like state through the blur of photos. I did pay the right amount and retrieve my credit card. Or did I? I don't recall the face or the name of the person who handed me the tickets. I don't recall if the person was a man or a woman, but I remember a blue shirt cuff, a whiff of citrus cologne. I responded correctly in Italian. This, I recall. The words come naturally, as if I've lived here all my life.

Inside the Pantheon, I stand in the center of what feels like a giant globe and look up at the oculus, at blue sky and clouds in transit. My father had walked with me around the perimeter to show how the sun cast white circles around the room at different times of day. I see one such circle poised over marble geometric forms, close to the tomb of Raffaello. I am alone here. Odd for this time of day. I open my purse to check the train tickets. I hold and count them in my hand before putting them back.

Tomorrow, I'll go to our cousin's jewelry store in Avezzano to try to pick up a gold charm, a *presentosa*, for Victoria's daughter Serena. She studies jewelry design and plans to wear it on a black, braided cord. *La presentosa* is a filigreed swirl of gold, two hearts in the center surrounded by triangle points resembling the rays of a star. A ribbon ties the two hearts together. My parents gave us each a *presentosa* on a charm bracelet for our sixteenth birthdays. The *presentosa* is also a circle, like the oculus, like the masonry globe I still stand in, unable to move. A few people walk around me. Their faint footsteps amidst the space and the silence keep pace with the memories which echo back.

They say Avezzano pales with respect to Rome. Let it pale. Let it not shout. Let it be the after-dinner *passeggiata* with my parents and my first night of love on the night of San Lorenzo. Let it be the first handknit dress with satin shoes, and the braided gold ring I now wear on my pinkie. It's where I imagine Mama laughing, young again, her resourcefulness on full display. What is it to return home? Those times with Mama and Papa. Victoria was older, but we both got measured by the *sarta* for dresses. Victoria didn't have the patience to stand while Cinzia wrapped the tape measure around her waist, chest, and arms. She was always fidgety. She wanted to play *calcio* with our male cousins. She tore her first pair of stockings.

Me, I snuggled my chubby arms inside the angora flounces. How soft they were, like clouds. I helped Mama tie the ribbons of lacy caps under my raised chin. She would tickle and I'd laugh and then came the hug. The hug she gave me each time. I was the most beautiful child in the entire world.

I couldn't wait for the creations that would emerge from Cinzia's rhapsodic fingers under my mother's tutelage. She tried to teach me. I now remember what I ignored back then: Deepen the darts on either side. Make sure there's no gap between shoulder blades. Measure the back waist length so the waist is not too high. It should sit right where the torso indents. We want to create what the French describe as *une belle poitrine.*

Armholes must hug the shoulder bone. The right skirt length matters. If off, it breaks the line. Hem by hand always. Drape the skirt over your knees; press, fold, and pin the fabric. Important most of all: Insert the threaded needle at an angle and pull the single thread through. Knot it at one end. Go slow. Listen as it slides so you know when to stop, so it doesn't pull. It's a subtle movement. Learn its sound. The stitches must be a row of even diagonals all around. When the hemming's done, lock the stitches with the double knot. Now smooth your hand over the finished hem like a caress. Before you buy a garment, turn it inside out, check for this precise hand stitching, not the machine kind. But it will never fit the same as when you make it yourself.

I no longer know how to hem. I send my clothes out to save time for mindless television shows and bursts of fabricated urgency. Now I remember her hands always at work. It was her relaxation, her separation from demons unseen by me. She needed nothing more than her sewing machine, the cloth in her hands, and the making of something beautiful for us. I didn't realize then how it fed her soul, enriched her mind, so she remains vital and lucid even now. All I've acquired and done over the years could never generate that kind of fullness and joy. Not the long tropical retreats, or the row of fanciful shoes and handbags, or the compliments of people I no longer see. I remember the stitches, the needle poised at the precise angle, the whisper of thread pulling through. Mostly, I remember the hands, hers and those of the *sarta,* accomplishing the magical: a perfectly even hem.

Lila

VITTORIA MASSAGES my feet and my hands as we rest in our hotel. Angela and Eva are asleep in the next room. I hear the cicadas outside and the music from the bar on the street. Ah, the silky laughter of youth. The journeys we pursue, the beauty we overlook and cast aside in our quest like pebbles on the beach, only to wish we could run back, gather them up again, and hold them close to our chests.

We leave for Avezzano in the morning. Already the chamomile tea is lulling me into a quiet sleep. She is an angel. She was my first, and she still stands at my side. She was born in Avezzano, so she knows what it was like before we sailed away on that glamorous ship, before the awe-inspiring thought of crossing that ocean by plane. I was not afraid, though. I wanted to fly away. I want to do that now. Fly away to meet my mother, Laura, in heaven and to have a good, hard talk with her.

The laughter outside grows louder. It is golden. It deepens. It shimmers inside me. As it did those nights, many nights, with Massimo, with others. I giggle at my own thoughts. I remember the scent of their British aftershaves and the silly things they said.

Of times when fear didn't interfere, when expectations didn't intervene. Should I tell all now?

"Open the window, Vittoria."

She pushes the large shutters out. How strong we felt at my mother's house in Antrosano every time as we pushed out with our arms to welcome in the sun, the sky, the smells of our earth, and the stars at night, the lunar magic of the moon.

Now, as Vittoria steps back, in front of our grand Roman window I see the corner of the *scalinata* awash with amber light from the streetlamps. The steeples and the white stone of Santissima Trinità dei Monti against a deepening cobalt sky. How beautiful it is. I want to jump up and dance, like that night, like so many nights. I remember squeezing Massimo's hand when we looked up at it. The perfume from the azaleas was strongest when closing their petals for the night.

"It's a bit chilly, Mama. Should I close the window a bit?"
I nod. "Si, *cara*. I just wanted one last look."

~

VICTORIA

WHEN WILL IT END? Three flights down in this huge, white, stone house is the *cantina* where Zia Adelina stores a mountain of almonds in their shells. It rises clear up to the garage ceiling, next to a smaller but no less daunting mountain of walnuts. Angela and I would climb and slide down both as kids. We were happy to crack the shells open all day long in exchange for one of Zia's *fritelle*.

Today at least a thousand almonds have been shelled and boiled. My fingers ache. Each time Zia dumps a pile in the center of the marble table, Lila digs in, rubs a dozen scalding almonds inside her palm until the skins peel away. She places them, glossy and smooth, in a pile beside me so I can cut them in half. She's watching. I make sure each cut is clean and even. I once bought slivered almonds and told her I'd peeled and cut them. No worries, I assured her. Boy, was I wrong. Mama slid the tasteless *crocccante* into the garbage. "Remember, Victoria, it takes as much time to do something right as it does to do it wrong. Do it right the first time so you don't have to redo it." The tantrum I threw when she told me to unravel half of the scarf I was knitting because I chose to disregard three dropped stitches. Never argue with a Lila, the only one of the *–inas* without an *–ina* attached to her name. Would that I had her patience now.

I look across the room at the French doors opening into the alcove into the room I stood inside when I was nine years old, holding onto Angela's hand. She was only two. The door to that room is closed, but I remember the day it was filled with lilies and roses and tears.

Zia dumps another pile of steaming hot almonds on the table. One scorches my hand, shock racing from my fingertips to my shoulder. I am at once short of breath, and then, surprisingly, I am calm. The heat subsides. I rub palms; the almond skins peel away willingly. I look at the closed door again. A sliver of light lines the bottom of the doorframe, and the glass sconces on the wall scatter the afternoon sunlight into rainbows. Warmth comes over me. I cut the almonds. They slice evenly. The haunting plays like music.

I think, Debussy's *La Mer*. I think, "Moon River." I think of the fluidity of water, of the *fontana* where Nonna Laura would gather water. How cold and clean it tasted.

Zia unloads the next steaming batch on the table.

"Ouch!" I check my palm for blisters.

"*Piano,*" says Mama, grabs her own handful, rubs them inside her palms, and drops the naked, shiny ones into a bowl. She grabs the next bunch, and I know there will be no stopping. My dreams of Debussy now sound more like a Jimi Hendrix guitar solo screeching me awake. But I keep working, harder and faster until we're done.

LAURETTA

Dear reader,

You are right to assume I was named after the esteemed Nonna Laura. It was my mother who named me so. No thoughts have been given toward me for a very long time because I died young.

I was born premature. My fragile lungs ill-prepared me for a voyage to Italy to see the family at eleven months old. In the middle of the night in a crib in Zia Adelina's bedroom, I started to cough. My chest hurt and it was hard to breathe, although I tried as hard as I could. Victoria picked me up. She smelled like violets. Her hands caressed my hair. She whispered soothing nonsense, but I sensed fear. Father was away in Rome with a mistress. Mother was asleep in the next room. Angela scrambled out of bed and watched Victoria anxiously pace the cold marble floors.

"Angela, get Mama."

I fell asleep in Mama's bed and in her arms that night already knowing I would not be returning to Astoria with my sisters.

I was considered the prettiest of the sisters because I'd inherited my mother's sweet little nose and father's huge dark eyes. Victoria was most attached to me and took care of me while Mama rolled out *sfoglia* for pasta at dawn, then caught the seven am subway to the garment district to turn out bathing-suit piecework. She took the job after they had to close the bakery. The few cents she earned for each hour were more carefully hidden than she was herself, hammered down in the evenings by my father's blows. He hadn't wanted a third child.

I died in Italy because I wanted to remain there. I was not destined to be part of the reality of men's hands, and when Nonna Laura held me for the first time, I knew myself home. I had a role to play in the unfolding of hardiness all the same. I guided my mother's hands when she worked. Move to the right, I said. Push the fabric slowly to the left now. Keep sewing. When you sew, you find joy, you have power. He can't hurt you then.

Mama was not the only one I bestowed my gifts onto. Onto Victoria, I painted humor. She commands the stage even when she least desires it, insecurity entangled with self-awareness. She has yet to define her next adventure, but re-invention is her strength. It is what has carried her through the *commedia,* the theater of her life.

Onto Angela, I gifted my mother's sartorial prowess. Not in the physical sense. Angela doesn't sew or knit or embroider. But she does so with her mind. I can't promise happy endings, because the world mosaic changes shape with each revolution of the sun, but as she crafts her own life, I would that she weaves words and confection. Poetry and prose and pastry cookbooks. Angela will struggle with confidence, with discipline and commitment because she loves to daydream and procrastinate. But procrastination is resistance's soft face. She is her mother's daughter.

I never knew Eva. Perhaps we could have been the closest because she is the most like me: floating over thoughts and emotions. For Eva, I bestow the largest of demands. She has drawn from all of us and has ventured beyond us. She'll stumble along the way. Eva is drawn to darkness. She knows where her demons lurk. She drinks too much, but that will stop. She will say once and for all—*I'm over it.* She will meet the love of her life in a migrant camp in a border town. She and her new lover will take in children separated from their parents, the sole survivors of families forced to flee their home.

Privilege blinds us to empathy. And empathy is the source of her power.

~

MY SISTERS now exit the back door of Nonna Laura's stone house. Its brown shutters are latched firm. Birds flutter around the tiled roof Laura and Franco chose to repair instead of replace. They stretched each lira as thin and as wide as one could.

The trio stop and look back. They don't speak. The air around them filters their words. With emotions this profound, there is no other way.

"This is what love feels like," whispers Victoria into the quiet dusk. This home, roots planted far under foot, gives sustenance while asking for little in return, only the most basic nourishment: water, nutrients, respectful tilling and planting, gestures that caress instead of extract.

Looking back, Angela focuses on the smaller house alongside. Victoria and Eva follow her gaze.

It is of native stone with a flat roof, this place where Laura gathered grapes to make the family's wine, which she stored in a giant barrel until it was ready for flasks on the dinner table. There, she and Franco brought hundreds of their own tomatoes for the annual *pommarola*. They washed and salted the tomatoes generously, then crushed, ground, and boiled them for hours before jarring them up to store in the *cantina*.

All year long, even in winter, opening a jar smelled like summer.

This small house was where grandparents hid food from the German soldiers. It was where daughters hid, too. Even then the vineyard provided refuge, nature protecting humans.

There are many rows, but the three sisters know which one leads from Nonna Laura's house to the long stone table in the clearing from which they can see the Apennines. It's early twilight. The vines seem smaller now, but Lamin, who arrived from Gambia twelve years ago, plucks the plump sticky grapes and nods. They are ready.

Sara and Emiliana, the new owners, supply grapes for the larger vineyards of Abruzzo. They greet Lila, who walks faster than the others, pushing branches away with her cane.

"One day, we should all go to Teramo and see the terroir there," says Angela, after all the greetings have been exchanged and the aroma of poured wine fills the air. "It is the same earth after all."

Teramo is not too many miles from Antrosano, and there in the larger vineyard, three popular wines are produced. Trebbiano, Montepulciano d'Abruzzo, and Cerasuolo. In past days, the *educazione* took place in front of those humble table wines, when Lila taught them where to place the knife, fork, and spoon on properly folded cloth napkins. One never used paper. It scratched the skin and was bad for the oceans.

Meanwhile, Papa made sure every glass stayed full. Angela takes his part now.

"In Japan, they say that if you fill your own glass, you have no friends."

"I'm always filling my own glass, so what does that say about me?" Eva turns her gaze toward the swirling branches inside the vines. Their chaos seems so effortless, so alive.

Lila, as if summoned by Bacchus from on high, rises to take the bottle from Angela and hands it to her youngest living daughter.

Eva understands what her mother is saying.

Stand up and fill your own glass. Wait for no one.

It's impossible not to see how the lines of worry have lifted from Lila's face. Her skin is luminous and smooth. This is something more than product or care. She is preparing to say goodbye.

"Thank you, Mama." Eva fills her glass first, then her mother's.

She will always take care of me, thinks Eva, even though she pretends not to. She won't let anyone know how scared I really am. The wine comforts and it tastes familiar, like the first time here so many years ago. By that time, she'd learned to sit far away from her father. It was the start. Even his shame and regret drew her even further away. He died unforgiven.

If she had forgiven him? Would it have changed anything?

"Not a chance," she says out loud and takes a longer sip.

"No more wine for you," Victoria misinterprets, on purpose.

Eva cups her hands around the glass tumbler. "After tonight I'm going to abstain for a while. I need to detox." She stares into the glass like a child searching for her goldfish. "Not just this. A bunch of stuff."

A dampness descends as the dank cognac of earthen fertility filters up around their ankles. The sky grays. A cool, feathery drizzle sprinkles hair and faces as Angela worries it will make her hair frizz, as Lila squares her shoulders thinking she can't run fast enough to protect her girls, as Victoria takes the antipasto platter and holds it out to Angela: *rollatine di salame e carciofi, prosciutto al coltello, sopresata, mortadella,* also rolled, this time into easy-to-grab cones; tiny stuffed artichoke hearts, roasted peppers, olives, twirled anchovies, each sprinkled with fresh-picked parsley; Mama's ineffable *erbetta*. At the end of every day and often in the middle, food was the salve that dressed wounds, sparked confessions, pulled open the curtains of self-delusion, and at times, popped the champagne cork for birthdays, passed exams, graduations, and all those affirmations we either leap or walk slowly towards.

The platter passes from hand to hand, each sister holding it two-handed for the next, as each recipient carefully takes all that she wants.

The platter makes the rounds several times. Sara brings out another: co-centric circles of *bruschetta di pomodoro* and *bruschetta con ventricina* sausage; crostini anointed with cannellini beans; fried zucchini flowers; finally, the hand-rolled gnocchi Lila had nicknamed her *talismano di gioia,* Their even shape, tiny pillows, are dressed with a *ragu* of meat, peas, and mushrooms. The sisters know what will follow: a platter of meats used for the sauce, along with dishes of *spinaci allessati, cavolfiore al umido,* broccoli rabe. All those vegetables Lila made delicious with nothing more than olive oil, water, and salt.

The sky shifts. Twilight emerges.

On each plate now each sister has her slices of prosciutto, chunks of *robiola,* a few roasted peppers jarred up every fall and still stored in the *cantina.* From one hand to the next, one plate to the next, the bottles making their rounds, bread broken. Olive oil fresh from the barrels. The rows, straight and even but tilting up toward Nonna Laura's house and the smaller house, where all this bounty was preserved and stored.

This is their mother's world, their father's world, the world of their ancestors. Around them and inside them is the DNA of their bone and their culture. Its voice carries on the wind as they enter more deeply into who they really are. A part of the landscape.

> *When we leave this earth, we are no longer flesh*
> *   and blood*
> *But we enter the flesh and blood of others, like*
> *   waters,*
> *Rivulets of streams,*

Rivers into a wider ocean.

So, the sisters will not speak of what they see and feel now, because how can they? It's as ethereal as Verdi's whispered voices in his *Requiem*.

Sara lights candles. Lamin pours the *vin santo*. Eva brings out plates of *cantucci* she made herself. Stars light up above them. I am there, and Nonna Laura is there. We are the two brightest stars hovering. Soon Lila will join. But for now, the Montepulciano d'Abruzzo made from their grapes releases their self-restriction and lets them speak.

"Thank you for making me come."

Why Lila speaks in English here, in this place, does not strike the sisters as strange.

"It did take convincing," Victoria laughs, using English also. Sara pours her a second glass of the Montepulciano d'Abruzzo. The liquid flashes with glints of raspberry in the light of a mellowing sun.

Lila lifts an elongated glass cappuccino cup, now repurposed as her personal wine glass. It's the only one she can lift and hold steady. She clinks it clumsily against Victoria's small tumbler.

"Cherries, roses, and spice, *salute!*"

There was no gulping it down, these grapes cultivated over centuries on this terroir under the mountainous shadow of Gran Sasso. No over-drinking. One lets the nectar permeate and recount its journey. They sip in silence, they laugh in harmony, their movements choreographed as if intended.

This was the way Lila wanted it; everything worked out as planned.

~

Epilogue: Lauretta

ONE YEAR LATER, the sisters return to Italy. This time, Lila is here with me and with Laura, and we three together follow their journey, dropping points on an illustrative map as an explorer might have drawn in the fourteenth century. We chart the course across oceans and terrain, amidst ancestral voices, amidst songs. Cultures intermingling in a single chorus. Lines and drawings scratch across parchment. The human journey interwoven with the nature encountered along the way.

They are here now, as per the trip organized by Eva, in the Boboli gardens of Florence to see Lorenzo Quinn's sculpture *Give.*

It's early morning, so the sky is grayish pink, and the green around them is lush and dark. Roses spread their petals and release their scent. The large white sculpture is of two hands, holding an olive tree between them. It will be here only for a short while and later it will travel to its permanent home in a sculpture garden in Pietrasanta. Eva reminds them of its global purpose, to inspire a salve for climate change, the work we achieve with crafty, generous hands.

In life to receive you have to give. And all of us have received and continue to receive much from the earth. Mine is meant to be a message of hope. The man's hand is mine, the woman's is a model's, their union represents all of humanity. White is the color of purity and innocence, of the dove and of peace. This is why I have chosen to offer an olive tree as a universal message.

— LORENZO QUINN

EPILOGUE

The Ear of Dionysius is a teardrop-shaped cave in the Parco Archeologico della Neopolis of southeastern Sicily. The painter Caravaggio named it so because of its otherworldly acoustics. Although sculpted of the limestone quarried here centuries ago, it curves up toward the sun like a ship's sail.

Soft, powdery earth molds to our feet as we follow intertwining trails in search of it. Along the way and even under the scorching heat, we fall prey to enchantment: cave houses chiseled into towering stone mountains, the remains of a Corinthian column, many delightful clusters of filmy leaves and stems speckled with wild capers spilling from solid rock. We rub the capers inside our fingers and wonder how such greens grow from dry stone. And why they taste so much better than any other capers we've eaten anywhere else in the world.

Beyond the Roman Theater, the creamy white co-centric circles of the Teatro Greco rise row by row high above the stage, as if striving to encircle the heavens. We continue our climb, undaunted, to the top, where the world as we know it falls away. Time and space are irrelevant. We are one with all of humanity. From here we look out to the vast shimmering expanse of the Ionian Sea.

We pay homage with our awe to the voices and rhythms of centuries past. We imagine, or do we hear?, the flow of discourse amongst spectators, past, present and future, dressed in their finest clothes and most uncomfortable shoes, programs in hand, expectations rising in anticipation, and the first swell of notes from the chorus, the first lines of a play by Aeschylus.

We descend the Teatro Greco and uncover the entrance to the Ear of Dionysius. A whisper of blue sky appears through a narrow, open tunnel far overhead. Although we'd perceived ourselves alone at the entrance to this mysterious grotto, inside we are no longer so. Feeling the presence of others around us in the dim, we walk, unperturbed, into total blackness. We know this is the right path. A truth will be revealed here.

And suddenly, voices. A choral group. People of varied ages and ethnicities emerge from the darkness. From where does this light suddenly come? They sing *"Va Pensiero"* from Verdi's *Nabucco*. The aria about people forced from their homes, about enslaved people, about wanderers seeking a better human response to cruelty and unrest.

And so, we sink into song, into these voices mingling with the voices of our ancestors, their ancestors, the ancestors of all humankind. We are walking the earth walked upon by the Hebrew slaves under Dionysius' tyrannical rule. And we are reminded that this too is our heritage, and our responsibility.

REFERENCES & RESOURCES

"Museo degli Innocenti: Entrepreneurs Who Donated Beauty Even to the Most Humble" by Stefano Albertini, La Voce di New York; June 28, 2020

The Films of Federico Fellini by Claudio G. Fava; Citadel Press, 1981.

Bottling the Past, Planting the Future: Immigrants in Italian Wine Production by Rebecca Marie Feinburg; Thesis and dissertation, UC Santa Cruz.

Brunelleschi's Dome by Ross King; Bloomsbury, 2000.

The work of Marta Mondelli at Festina Lente Home.

The work of Carlos Huber at Arquiste fragrances.

ACKNOWLEDGMENTS

That Time of Day coalesced into that metaphorical moment when the voices of so many courageous, creative, and socially conscious people formed a chorus in my mind.

The first among these is my husband, Steve. Thank you for believing in me, in this book, in strong women who deserve to have their stories told, and in social justice for all humankind.

The second among these is my daughter, Daniela, who makes us proud, brings us joy, and reminds us every day, along with our son-in-law Paul, of the work we need to do to create a better world for future generations.

Whether through conversation or via collaboration, each of the following individuals has defined and shaped the protagonists of my stories and their journeys.

Publisher and mentor, Cheryl Benton. Your creativity, indomitable spirit, and commitment to writing and publishing women's stories brought this collection into the world. How fortunate I am that our paths have crossed and crisscrossed over the years. You continue to motivate and inspire me.

Developmental editor, cover designer, and irrepressible muse Catherine Michele Adams. Your photographer's eye and razor-sharp insight found the edges and contours inside in each narrative moment. You guided my hand with unflappable clarity and grace, as if I were holding a paintbrush or a sculptor's chisel.

Writer/teacher Edi Giunta and the generous, talented writers and poets of Edi's Shooting Stars. Thank you, thank you, thank you for welcoming me into this community and for teaching me to mine the stories of my ancestors. There is more to come.

Louise DeSalvo. We have never met but your literary works, including *The Art of Slow Writing* and collaborations with Edi Giunta, continue to give voice to Italian-American women.

And the women of the NY Leadership Council for Plan International, chaired by Cheryl Benton. Your efforts on behalf of girls in the developing world have taught me many lessons on what is possible and why our privilege is not a right but a responsibility.

I convey a special thank you to the accomplished readers, reviewers, thinkers, creators, and activists from around the globe who inspire me every day: Flavia Brunetti, Susan Harvey, Dr. Marie-Elena Liotta, Phyllis Melhado, Marilyn Wilson, and Angela Vitaliano. You draw on your strength, creative gifts, and love of humankind to pay it forward with dedication and imagination, shot through with a wink of irreverence along the way.

I thank my unflappable cheerleaders Bert and Maria and my extended family on both sides of the ocean: Your encouragement saw me through writer's block time and time again.

I also give thanks to the mountains, hill towns, and resplendent castles of my home region of Abruzzo and to my cousins and family members who still gather and recount the enchanting stories of our ancestors.

I thank my fabulous, fearless, and unstoppable women friends, you know who you are.

I thank my ancestors who re-directed my path when I wandered off course. I know you are guiding me still.

I thank Marta Mondelli, actress, writer, director and founder of Festina Lente Home in Milan.

I thank Federico Bonechi and the team at Palazzo San Niccolò in Florence

My Italian heritage gives thanks always for Casa Italiana Zerilli/Marimò of New York University and for all New York Italian Women. You keep that heritage not only alive but actively living.

And finally, as always, I give loving thanks to my parents, Clelia and Umberto.

ABOUT THE AUTHOR

Gabriella Contestabile is an author, educator, and the founder of SU MISURA JOURNEYS, a boutique travel company connecting people to the artisans of Florence. She emigrated from Italy to Ottawa in 1953 and to New York City in 1959 where she currently resides with her husband. In her pre-writer life as a foreign language teacher, management development specialist, and a fragrance/cosmetics executive, she visited the fields and perfume laboratories of Grasse and worked in a family-owned perfumery in Florence. It was there that her passion for perfume and artisanship took hold. Gabriella is a strong advocate of the arts, of multiculturalism, and of social justice—a passion inspired by reading Dickens, Dante, and Louisa May Alcott at a very young age.

The Artisan's Star: A Novel

Elio Barati's perfumery shop in Florence marks its entrance with a mosaic star. This shop immerses Elio in the artisanal world he loves, but he harbors a regret. As a young man he created a full-fledged perfume of jasmine, iris, and cypress at the renowned École des Parfumeurs in Grasse—a fragrance his idealism and stubbornness boxed away before ever bringing it to light.

A second star now brightens Elio's life, his daughter Romina, an artist. She has her father's unrealized talent, a precise and intuitive sense of smell. She's also inherited more challenging traits of Elio's: unbridled ambition and an insatiable wonder for the world.

But changes ripple through modern-day Florence. Artisan traditions wane; and when Romina tells her father she has no intention of running the family business Elio fights to hold on to the Florence he cherishes. Confronting the lost opportunities of his youth, Elio is thrust into this journey by five spirited women: his Greek mother, Elena; his mentor Palma; his soul mate, Marina; his astronomer wife, Sofia; and finally his beautiful artist daughter, who like the city of her birth, shows him how tradition and modernity can and must co-exist.

Now he must alter his own path by harnessing the transformative powers of the fine and artisanal arts.

Sass, Smarts, and Stilettos: How Italian women make the ordinary, extraordinary

How do Italian women turn the ordinary into extraordinary? Why do their lives seem less complicated, but more complete and alluring?

Discover what's behind this seductive ethos of effortless chic, and how to live an extraordinary and stylish life, all' italiana.

Sass, Smarts, and Stilettos is not just a celebration of Italian women, but of all women; of their innate ability to think outside the box, to make magic from mayhem, and to have a wild good time doing it.

In the words of our Italian grandmothers, "Forza!"

PRAISE FOR SASS, SMARTS, AND STILETTOS

"An Italian lifestyle is understated, not loud, it doesn't need to brag, because it's an inherited patrimony, made of the simple things, yet luxurious and sophisticated, a tribute to quality. Gabriella does an exquisite and ambitious job at describing it in passionate detail, and in a book you won't want to put down."

— FRANCESCA BELLUOMINI, AUTHOR
OF *THE CHEAT SHEET OF ITALIAN STYLE*